CORNERO'S GOLD

LARRY O'BRIEN

Illustrations by Liam O'Brien

A Novel

RIVER GROVE
BOOKS

Published by River Grove Books
Austin, TX
www.rivergrovebooks.com

Distributed by River Grove Books

Design and composition by Greenleaf Book Group
Cover design by Greenleaf Book Group
Cover Images: © iStockphoto/Thirteen-Fifty and © iStockphoto/lucky-photographer
Interior illustrations by Liam O'Brien

Publisher's Cataloging-in-Publication data is available.

Print ISBN: 978-1-63299-713-5

eBook ISBN: 978-1-63299-714-2

First Edition

This book is dedicated to my lovely late wife, Jacqueline. She was my lover, my companion, my friend, and my muse. Without her support and encouragement, this book would never have come to be. I would also like to dedicate my novel to my friend, mentor, and fellow PI, Nils Grevillius, whose own literary efforts inspired me to give it a try myself.

PROLOGUE

1939

On a moonlit night in July of 1939, a large white ship lay anchored three miles off of Manhattan Beach on the Southern California coast. Its large neon sign, saying *SS Rex*, could be seen from the shore, beckoning wannabe gamblers to take the short taxi ride out beyond the three-mile limit. The deep waters of Santa Monica Bay were calm, as they typically were this time of year, and the waves lapped gently and harmlessly at the sides of the vessel. Considering the late hour, most of the gamblers had returned ashore for the night. However, since the last of the night's water taxis were still shuttling almost silently on the glassine waters between the ship and the shore, a motor launch with its running lights off and six men aboard approached the ship largely unnoticed, cutting the engine as they slipped alongside.

After they boarded, they spread out as if by design. Two of the men overpowered the watch. They remained at the gangway as lookouts, while their four comrades entered the main gambling deck.

Only a few gamblers remained. The gambling deck was long and wide; it took up the entire center of the ship. There was a dance floor and well-stocked bar and restaurant on the top deck. It provided a place for the non-gamblers to relax and spend their money. But the gambling gallery was the moneymaker and was not elaborately decorated—it was simply a place where people went to lose their money. Along the starboard side stood a row of gleaming slot machines and a second, somewhat smaller bar, stocked principally with hard liquor to fortify the gamblers' bravado. The port side mirrored the same arrangement, and the broad, smoky center of the gallery featured roulette, craps, blackjack, and various other gambling tables. At the far end of the casino area was the entrance to the counting room, only partially concealed by elaborate draperies hanging on either side. That's where the four intruders headed, trying not to draw attention to themselves. They lingered casually outside the entrance, waiting for one of the staff to approach the door. They didn't have to wait long.

The unlucky individual was none other than Nick Colleti—who was on duty as the general floor supervisor on the *Rex* that night. That meant that he was in charge of keeping a close eye on the dealers and pit bosses; making sure the proceeds were going into the establishment's coffers and not into the croupiers' pockets. As it so happened, Nick approached the door of the counting room just as it was getting close to closing time, when the evening's take would be counted up. He just reached the door when a gunman stuck the barrel of a 1911 .45 Colt in his ribs.

"Don't say a word," the gunman said in a low, gruff tone. "If you know what's good for you, you'll act like nothing's wrong and you'll get us inside."

Nick followed his instructions to the letter, knocking his familiar knock on the door—whoever was working on the other side needed to unlock the otherwise impenetrable door so that those on the outside could gain entry.

Inside the counting room, Jack O'Banion, Tony Cornero's accountant and silent partner in the ownership of the *Rex*, approached the door to flip the locks, fully expecting to see Nick on the other side. But the instant the door swung open, the four intruders rushed their way into the room with guns drawn, pushing Nick headlong in front of them, a gun at his back.

The guy who'd been doing all the talking barked out another order. "Everybody but those counting the money get your hands in the air. And don't try anything funny!"

He then ordered the men counting the money to gather it up and put it in bags, coins and all. Along with the paper money, there were stacks of silver dollars and other coins from the slots. But the main target was the vault, a basic combination lock safe embedded in the wall at the far end of the counting room. The leader then motioned with his pistol to O'Banion and ordered him to open it up.

Inside the vault was the jackpot. There, in thirty-six nice little wooden crates just waiting to be heisted, were seventy-two bars of gold, each crate weighing over fifty pounds. Again, he motioned to O'Banion and the four men who had been counting the night's receipts.

"Load those crates onto those dollies and take them to the gangway," he said.

While the leader supervised the transfer of the gold to the waiting speedboat, his three comrades rounded up the casino staff and the remaining customers. Though everyone was panicked, they cooperated the way most people do when they have a bunch of gun barrels pointed at them, hands aloft and shuffling like nervous sheep in whatever direction they were ordered to go. The captives were taken to the lower deck known as the bilge, where they were locked up in one of the several utility rooms that lined the dark hallway in the bottom of the ship.

The small band of robbers must have been pleased. Everything went without a hitch, like a successful and well-planned military operation. They were in and out in less than an hour, and without firing a shot. And minutes after the gold and the rest of their booty had been loaded onto the waiting boat, they were speeding off into the darkness of night and what they believed would be the anonymous safety of the open sea. But it wasn't going to be so easy.

Back on the gambling ship, Jack O'Banion sounded the claxon, the ship's alarm system, calling to general quarters any of the casino staff who might not have had the misfortune to be locked up. The alarm also summoned the sailing crew—the sailors responsible for piloting and operating the white ship—and most importantly, Captain Pete, the white ship's sailing master. As he did this, Nick Colleti raced below decks to free all of those who had been locked in the bilge. That included Nick's brother, Tommy Colleti, the other half of the brotherly team of iron-fisted strongmen responsible for overseeing the gambling deck.

"Grab a launch," Jack barked at the now freed sailors. "Nick, you're going after them, you and Tommy and Pete—take three men with you and go get our money back. I'll stay here and get things put back together."

"Aye, boss," Nick said.

The Colleti brothers joined Captain Pete and the three sailors aboard the launch. They immediately cast off and went after the pirates, who by now had a hefty head start. They headed in the same general direction that the pirates had, which was in a southwesterly direction toward the northern tip of Catalina Island, hoping against all odds to catch them quickly.

No such luck was to be had. Captain Pete could only follow his instincts. Once the thieves were out of sight, they could have gone anywhere. They could have turned east toward the peninsula or turned north toward Malibu. Heading toward Catalina was his only real choice. It was an exhausting process as they had to keep their eyes peeled for a glimpse of the pirates' boat the entire time. Occasionally, with the help of the moonlight, Captain Pete thought he caught sight of a glinting blip of white water on the horizon, the absconding boat's wake, he imagined.

"Is that them?" Nick asked, desperation in his voice.

"I don't know," Pete replied, "but it's the only hope we got."

Things were looking grim when, at about eight in the morning, just off the north end of the island, they finally caught up with the fleeing pirates. The captain's instincts had served him well. Theorizing the pirates might try to use Catalina for cover, he reasoned they could go north of the island and turn south to try to make their final escape, or they could go south of the island and turn north. He guessed the latter, and he guessed right.

Coming up surprisingly quickly on the pirates' boat, Tommy Colleti grabbed a submachine gun and fired off a few rounds. Much to everyone's shock, the bullets must have hit a fuel line, because the fleeing boat immediately caught fire and then, only seconds later, there was a massive explosion. The ensuing flash, though brief, was blinding. Even at their relatively safe distance they could feel the thudding concussion from the blast and the intense heat that followed it. Burning wreckage fell everywhere, some even landing on the pursuers' boat.

Captain Pete barked orders to his crew as everyone scrambled to get the burning debris off the boat deck. Their drift on the current carried them right into the path of the noxious smoke from the burning wreck, so thick that the men aboard the boat couldn't see two feet in front of them, which only added to the chaos.

When the smoke cleared, all that was left of the boat with the six intruders and all of that gold was some burning debris floating on the surface of the water. The pirates and their boat had disappeared in an instant, right before their eyes. Captain Pete motored cautiously toward the wreckage to look for survivors, Nick Colleti holding his .45 at arm's length vigilantly in case there were, but none were found.

Like any good navigator, Pete had been taking notes in his head on bearings, time spent in each direction, and the speed of their boat. Later when they returned to the *Rex*, the captain was able to plot the location of the wreck, writing it down on a nautical chart of the region off Catalina. All was duly noted in the ship's log so that they could go back and dive for the missing gold with the hope of recovering some, if not all, of it.

Jack O'Banion was fit to be tied. How was he going to explain what happened to his partner, Tony Cornero, when Tony returned to the *Rex* the following afternoon, back from one of his frequent business trips to Las Vegas? Even worse, how were both of them going to explain to Jack Dragna, a local LA mobster, that the million-plus-dollar shipment of gold they were babysitting for the Sicilian mafia had been stolen right out from under them? This would not sit well with the Sicilians, who lived by a cardinal rule: What belongs to the organization belongs to the organization. Tony and Jack knew they would be held responsible for it. Sooner or later, the organization would collect the debt that Jack and Tony now owed them. Although they took no immediate action against Tony or Jack—which was surprising—this event would hang over both of them for the next sixteen years like a dark cloud.

The Colleti brothers give chase.

CHAPTER 1

1974

A t around two on a Friday afternoon, I was at my desk in the trading room of Security Pacific Bank, staring out the south-facing window, gazing longingly at Catalina Island, barely visible on the distant horizon. I was thinking about the cold beer that I was determined to have over at Stepps after work, when Kathy, the position clerk, yelled over to me.

"Kit, it's for you. It's your father on 05."

I picked up the handset and said, "Hi, Pop, what do you need?"

"Oh, just for you to come by the office after work," he said. "Your package has arrived. Let's open up a couple cold ones. Oh, and also, I have a new client and I'd like you to be there for the meeting."

"Sure. See you in about an hour and a half," I said and hung up.

The package was a case of Czechoslovakian Michelob that Pop and I had shipped over from Germany. Normally, the last thing I wanted to do on a Friday afternoon was go by Pop's detective agency in Pasadena, especially considering what was waiting for me over at Stepps, where I had pretty much unlimited access to some really good tavern-style food and drink, thanks to an open tab from a broker benefactor. But now there was a special brew waiting for me at his office, so I had a little incentive.

Pop was a former LAPD cop turned private investigator. He now had a decent agency going in Pasadena. In addition to being a foreign exchange trader, I'd been working off and on for Pop as one of his operatives since I was in college. I'd made more money working for him repossessing cars and as a wheel man than I ever did working in the mail room at the bank, and it was all cash under the table. I'd saved enough to pay cash for my 1968 Mustang Shelby GT, the BULLITT model.

Pop was now around seventy-three and still very much in charge. He looked good for his age, and everybody guessed him at about sixty. My hope was that he had passed down those great genetics and I would look that good—and be that sharp—when I was his age.

I loved working for my dad as a private eye, but the pay at the bank was so much better now that I had advanced up the ranks to the foreign exchange department, especially when you factored in the bonuses. Don't get me wrong, Pop was doing very well, but he had other employees, some with families that truly needed the paycheck a lot more than I did, so at some point, a couple of years ago, I began to do all my work for him pro bono.

And sometimes for fun.

I pulled into the parking lot about 3:30 and took the elevator to the second floor, then ambled down the dim hallway to the door of his office. The whole place looked right out of a noir detective movie, as cliché as that might sound. The building was turn-of-the-century, in Old Town Pasadena, and the frosted glass in the door read Triangle Investigations.

Pop had originally set the agency up with two of his police

buddies: Hughie Carr, his partner, and another cop named Al Sherman. Their intent was to work at the agency part-time and keep their day jobs as cops, at least until they got it off the ground. But fate stepped in to adjust those plans. They had no sooner got their doors open when the Japanese attacked Pearl Harbor and war was declared. Like many other police officers, Pop, Hughie, and Al were either drafted or volunteered for service. Pop volunteered, sort of. Actually, he more than volunteered; during the first "dustup" in Europe, he lied about his age, joined up with the Navy at age fifteen, and celebrated his sixteenth birthday on a "tin can" chasing German subs around the Atlantic. So, having been in the Navy during the First World War and becoming a seasoned police detective between the wars, Uncle Sam decided he would be of better use in Naval Intelligence than he would catching bad guys on the streets of LA. Needless to say, the agency's launch was put on hold until the end the war.

Except, when the war was over, Hughie and Al decided to retire from law enforcement altogether and pursue other careers. Pop decided to go it alone and opened the agency anyway. He worked it part-time as he originally intended and by 1954, he had his thirty years in as a cop, so he could retire with a full pension and focus all of his talent and energy on the agency. He kept the original name to honor his friends.

I opened the door to the anteroom and approached the receptionist's desk. Sitting there was his new office manager—none other than Jacquie herself.

Wow, I thought, *Pop really pulled it off, didn't he?* Here sitting before me was the blonde, blue-eyed, drop-dead gorgeous woman I had known since she and I were kids.

Of course, this wasn't our first reunion, though our last one had been cut short just as things were beginning to heat up—I had reunited with her six months ago, however briefly, and it was at that point that I realized she wasn't a kid anymore. I was starting to fall for her big time, then life got in the way. I couldn't believe it! I'd been asking about having her brought up—hiring her to work at the agency, I mean—time and time again, and had little response from Pop about it. And now, here she was. It appeared that Pop had been listening after all and had evidently brought her to LA from Indio, where she had been working for the Riverside County Sheriff. Now that she was here, perhaps we could resume our friendship—if she was willing, that is. *Thanks, Pop*, I said to myself. I would have to remember to do something nice for the old guy.

"Hi, babe!" I said, approaching her desk, squinting as if hard of seeing. "Is it really you?"

She laughed good-naturedly. "Yup, it sure is," she said.

Behind her stood a row of filing cabinets, a new copy machine, and a fax. Pop was going high-tech. An overstuffed couch opposite the desk provided seating for potential clients, but since there was no one waiting, I assumed our new client hadn't arrived yet, and that allowed me a few moments to focus on Jacquie. "It's been way too long. I wasn't sure when I'd see you again."

"I know what you mean. I felt the same way," she said. "But thanks to your dad, I'm here now."

"This is true," I said, "and now that you are here, I'm not going to let you out of my sight."

"I hope not," she said. "I was going to call you up and tell you, but I thought just showing up would be a nice surprise."

"Nice is the understatement of the year," I said.

After a little more small talk, we agreed to meet later that night for dinner. It was time to see Pop, and those specially imported beers.

Flanking the filing cabinets were two doors. The one on the

left was to Pop's private office, the one to the right of the cabinets opened into what was originally supposed to be a filing room/conference room combo. Instead, Pop had turned it into a recreation area of sorts, with a little bar and a pool table squeezed into it. There was a large picture window facing Colorado Boulevard with a tattered leather couch in front of it—oddly facing toward the window, until one realized that was where we watched the parade every year.

I went into Pop's private office, where he sat behind a huge oak desk in front of a similarly sized window that also faced Colorado Boulevard. There was a big executive chair for him, and arrayed in front of his desk were four club-style chairs for clients. Two long, matching mahogany credenzas stood along the back wall on either side of the anteroom door. Above one of them hung a matte painting of LA at night—it was an original from a former client who had given it to Pop in lieu of cash payment. On the other was a 1/24-scale model of Pop's sloop the *Black Widow*, and on the wall above that was a taxidermied swordfish Pop had caught off Catalina. On the opposite wall was yet another credenza and another stuffed fish.

I always felt at home in his office. I'd been present every time Pop added another trophy to the wall, and every stuffed fish had a memory attached. And of course, the model of the *Black Widow* brought back countless memories.

The *Widow* was Pop's labor of love. When Pop was discharged from the Navy after World War I, he settled in San Diego and became a house painter. He had developed a love for the sea and boats somewhere along the way—strange considering he was born in Cripple Creek, Colorado, a turn-of-the-century mining camp, and later raised in Rhyolite, Nevada, where his father was a deputy sheriff—what was essentially the "Old West." But I digress.

He had built the *Widow* by hand with the help of some buddies and a ton of serious elbow grease. She was a shiny forty-foot-long sloop and acquired the name from her coloring. Glossy black hull, white superstructure, with gray decks. A strip of gold paint separated the hull line from the superstructure. On the stern was painted a black widow spider displaying that telltale red dot.

In the early years of Prohibition, Pop supplemented his income from painting houses by running a little bootleg whiskey in from Mexico. When she was all finished, he used the swift-sailing *Widow* to bring the goods in by sea.

Pop was essentially a bootlegger by trade. But—here's the funny part—he'd had enough by 1924 and switched sides, joining the San Diego Police Department. He then met and married his first wife, Gladys, who gave him a lovely daughter in 1925. That marriage was over by 1930 and after the divorce, Gladys moved to New York, taking their daughter Patsy with her.

In 1933, he met his second wife, Edna, my mom, and her daughter Kay from her first marriage. They fell in love, got married, and when, in 1935, he got a job offer from the Los Angeles Police Department, on a track to become a detective, he took it. He packed up his new family, boat and all, and moved to LA. Nine years later, I arrived.

Needless to say, I practically grew up on the *Black Widow*. I think it was a combination of hearing Pop's tales of the old days and being around such a beautiful boat that I developed my own love for the sea. That and maybe a few old Errol Flynn pirate movies.

Pop lifted his hand in greeting and directed me to the fridge.

"The beer's in there. Grab one for me too," he said.

"Thanks, Pop—and I don't mean just for the beer," I said with a smile and a nod toward the anteroom.

"You're welcome," he said with an "I gotcha" look on his

rugged face and a mischievous glint in his piercing blue eyes. "I thought you'd enjoy my little surprise. It took some major doing but I finally convinced her to come on board. And I wasn't just doing you a favor—she'll be a good fit to our organization."

"She will indeed. In more ways than one," I said with a devilish grin.

"I'm sure," Pop said. "I'm just happy to see you happy. You've got a grin going that stretches from one ear to the other."

I fetched the beer, and we toasted the new arrangement.

Moments later, our new client walked in. Much to my surprise, it was my Uncle Jack and his lawyer, Albert Lowenstein, followed by the ever-present Max. Max Di Marco. He was Uncle Jack's long-time driver, bodyguard, and all-around "Mr. Fixit." He wasn't exactly a handyman—I never saw him do so much as replace a defective light switch or use a plunger to unclog a stopped-up toilet—so we never knew what the specifics of his actual job entailed. But he was also a devoted, loyal friend, to the point of being part of our extended family.

Uncle Jack was only a year older than Pop but looked much older—he had a worn-down look to him despite the fact that he was wearing a tasteful three-piece pin-striped suit. His hair was gray and thinning and, compared to his two companions, he was on the skinny side. Max was about twenty years younger, medium height, and on the stocky side. His hair was full, neatly cropped, and dark black. On this occasion he was wearing a leather jacket, a white turtleneck sweater, and slacks—a stylish kind of guy, in a roguish sort of way.

Albert Lowenstein, by contrast, was a corpulent fellow, with short, cropped graying hair. He spoke with a slight British accent that seemed to have diminished over the years. According to Pop, "Fat Albert" came to the US to study law. He liked it here so much that he decided to become a citizen, and he immigrated to the US just before the war. He always reminded me of Sydney Greenstreet in *The Maltese Falcon*—the resemblance was uncanny. He too was wearing a tailored navy-blue pin-striped suit. He was known as Al or Albert to his closest friends, Mr. Lowenstein to people of my status, and "Fat Albert" behind his back—he had just the right combination of sleaze and class and arrogance to make him one of the most successful criminal lawyers around. He had been Uncle Jack's and Pop's lawyer for as long as anyone could remember.

When everyone was seated, Pop began going over the plan. "The assignment's pretty straightforward. Jack wants us to deliver an envelope to the address provided and pick up a package in return. Our contact's name is R. Ricotta, like the cheese—probably not his real name. The address is over on Mt. Washington. You, Kit, will be making the delivery. You can get the address from Jacquie when you pick up the envelope here on Monday. The meeting for the exchange is set for 6:00 p.m."

Sounded simple enough, and I was assured there was nothing to it.

Yeah, right—there was rarely "nothing to it."

"Mind if I ask what's in the envelope, and what I'll be picking up?" I asked.

"Yes," Fat Albert said emphatically. "The less you know, the better. That's why I'm hiring you and keeping your Uncle Jack out of it. This gives you attorney-client privilege on anything you might happen to hear or discover during your . . . let's just call it your 'mission.'"

"Ohhh-kay," I said, drawing out the syllables. I didn't like all the secrecy, but sometimes you have to work with what you get, and Pop seemed okay with it.

Pop continued, "As I said, you can pick up the envelope on Monday afternoon. And now Jack, Al, and I have other business to discuss."

"Great," I said, eagerly taking my cue to take my leave.

"So, until then, the weekend is yours," he said with a wink and a nod toward the outer office.

"Extra great. Mind if I shag a sixer of the Mickeys for dinner tonight?" I asked as I got to my feet.

"Nope. Take a couple," he replied.

With that our meeting ended, or at least my part of it, so I went out to have a little chat with Jacquie.

"So . . . lemme guess. It took a lot of convincing to get you to come up here?" I said with a wink and a grin. "Pop have to twist your arm?"

"Not really. I just played hard to get, so he'd make me a great offer. And he did. Especially after he pointed out the benefits," she said with a big, provocative grin.

"Copy that," I said. "You'll have to fill me in later on all of those."

"Let's make later sooner," she said. Since it was about quitting time, she clocked out and grabbed her purse.

Eager to please—and still in disbelief at our fortuitous reconnection—I escorted her to her car. Since we had decided earlier that neither of us wanted to go out, we decided to have dinner at my place. So I gave her a key and directions to my apartment.

"See you in a few," I said as I kissed her goodbye. "I'm going to the store to grab a couple of steaks and some salad fixings. Do you mind taking this beer and putting it on ice for me? I don't want it to get warm while I'm at the store. I'll see you at my place. Oh, and if you don't mind, the charcoal and stuff to start the hibachi are on the balcony—see if you can get the fire going. No sweat if not."

"Will do," she said and started her car. It was like we hadn't skipped a beat, and that was fine by me.

I just smiled as I watched her pull out of the garage. *Wow*, I thought to myself. *What a difference a day makes.*

Pop and company discuss the case.

CHAPTER 2

I stopped at Ralph's Supermarket to pick up the food and grab a good Merlot. By 5:30 p.m., I was turning left into the underground garage of my apartment building. I could see Jacquie on my balcony. She was sitting on a lounge chair tending to the hibachi. By the looks of it, she had already met my roommate Fred—he was sitting on her lap to get his tummy rubbed. Oh— Fred was a fat ball of fur disguised as a black-and-white tuxedo cat. I'd gotten him as a kitten from a friend at work, and he'd kindly condescended to share *his* apartment with me.

I parked my car in the usual spot, picked up my mail, and went up to my apartment. It was a great place, one of only three in the building that had a working fireplace, and the only one with a balcony. The owner was another client who owed us, so I'd gotten a good deal. Detective work is often like that. You find yourself working with people who are mostly good, who've been screwed by other people who aren't so good, and who tragically have little or no money to pay people like my father and me to help them out of a fix. So, they pay you in other ways.

Anyway, I opened the front door, sat my groceries down on the floor, tossed my keys in the dish on the little table near the entry, and started to check the mail in my hand. Right on cue, Fred ran inside from the balcony and plopped himself on top of everything, wanting to be petted. I picked him up, gave him a perfunctory hug, and dropped him onto the floor, whereupon he hissed at me and went back to Jacquie. "Traitor," I muttered, as I tossed the mail in the dish for later, picked up the groceries, and went into the living room.

The fireplace was on the right wall surrounded by a built-in bookcase that showcased my stereo components, records, all of my books from college, and my noir detective library with all the greats: Chandler, Hammett, and Ross Macdonald. Partly because Pop was a detective, but mostly because of those books, I'd always wanted to be a detective. Kind of explains why nowadays, I was willing to do this work pro bono.

The living room had an overstuffed leather chair with its back to the dining room. Against the faux brick back wall was the leather couch. On the wall above the couch was an array of black-and-white photos that I had taken over the years. Perched in the corner where the sliding doors met the fireplace wall was a brand-new color TV that actually had decent color. The front wall was all sliding doors, opening up onto the balcony that now held my wonderfully unexpected guest.

A counter separated the dining room from the kitchen where I stood. I watched as Jacquie came in from the balcony. Boy, did she look pretty. I sat the groceries on the counter of the galley-style kitchen and gave her a big hug and a kiss.

"That will have to hold you until later," I said.

"Maybe, maybe not," she said with a wink.

She took the steaks, chilled the Merlot, and started to prepare a salad. It felt like no time had passed since we'd last been together. I moseyed on down the hall to the bedroom to change into my jeans, tennies, and a T-shirt.

I looked around the space and hoped Jacquie would approve. The bedroom had the same faux brick treatment as the living room. The bed had been constructed in a modern style, with a low headboard with built-in side tables that had some books on them, whatever I happened to be reading at the time. In this case, it was *The Onion Field* by Wambaugh. There was also an articulating reading lamp for lighting. Above the headboard were more black-and-white photos. On the side table was my alarm radio and the telephone, which had a thirty-foot cord so I could take it just about anywhere in the apartment. I grabbed it, out of force of habit, and went back to the kitchen, trailing the cord on the floor behind me and hoping that Fred wouldn't start chasing after it, as he so often did.

When I arrived, the steaks had been properly seasoned. I popped another beer and poured Jacquie a glass of Merlot, as she finished the salad.

"To the beginning of a beautiful friendship," I said in my best Bogey imitation.

"To us," she said, nodding in agreement as we clicked wine glass to bottle in a toast.

We put the steaks on. Dinner was perfect. I had my steak blood-rare, she had hers medium. I decided to put some music on the stereo to set the mood. I picked out one of my favorite albums by Dinah Washington. The first song that played was "What a Difference a Day Makes." I couldn't help thinking how appropriate it was.

As I said, I'd known Jacquie for a long time. Her dad and mine were Navy buddies. Her father owned a bar in La Quinta where my parents had a weekend retreat. Their home was next door.

Jacquie was seven years younger than me. When I graduated from college and went into the Navy, she was just a gawky kid starting high school. By the time I returned, she had graduated, moved to Washington State, gotten married, had a kid, and gotten divorced and moved back to La Quinta with her baby son, Nick, in tow. There she proceeded to get her life together. She got in with the Riverside County Sheriff's Department as a dispatcher.

Six months ago, I was down in La Quinta working on a case. I ran into her at a place called the Cove, a popular bar that her dad owned and operated, where she was helping out by waiting tables on her days off. I quickly realized she wasn't a gawky kid any-more—you know, being the astute detective that I am. Seriously though, far from it—she had transformed into a beautiful woman, and her bright personality had only blossomed. I think we both felt an instant connection.

She was more than happy to use her position at the Sheriff's Department to help me obtain the information I needed for my investigation. I purposely took longer than I needed, just so I could spend more time with her. Maybe we both got cold feet or something, I don't know, but we decided that the logistics of where we lived and worked would be too much, so we parted. I told my dad, half kidding, that he should hire her and bring her to LA. He just laughed and said, "You never know." I brought it up a couple more times before I gave up and let it drop.

I hadn't seen her again until today in the anteroom of my dad's office. He had told me he was hiring a new office manager, but he'd never said who and I hadn't bothered to ask.

After dinner we moved the conversation to the couch. As we sat down, Jacquie asked me, "So what's the new case about? Or can you not tell me?"

"Well," I said, "you do work for the company now, and you'll read any reports that are filed, so I can tell you everything. Problem is, there isn't much to tell. Uncle Jack, or should I say Fat Albert, since he's the client, wants me to deliver a package to a fella over on Mt. Washington and pick up another package from him. What's in each package I've not been told. Apparently, that is 'need to know.' It's supposed to be a standard drop and should be a piece of cake. Of course, I've heard that before. But that's all there is and now you know everything I know."

"Um," she said, "sounds like you'll be safe enough, not that I'm worried or anything."

"I appreciate your concern," I said, "but this isn't my first rodeo, and you've known me for a while."

"Yes, I have, and that's what worries me." She laughed.

I just shrugged and gave her a dumb grin.

"Let's talk about something else," I said. "I have the whole weekend free, and I'm planning on going surfing tomorrow. Would you like to go along?"

"I can't. I have no one to take care of Nick," she said. "In fact, I'm going to have to leave in a little while to relieve my mom. She's taking care of him now."

"Understood," I said. "Would you like to go sailing next weekend?"

"I'd love to," she said. "I just have to arrange a sitter for Nick."

"If you can't get anyone, I'm sure my Mom and Pop wouldn't mind filling in," I said.

"That would be great," she said. "I'll let you know."

It was a date then. After a few more hours of getting *reacquainted*, she had to leave. The evening had gone by much faster than I had wanted it to, but you know what they say about time flying when you're having fun. I cleaned up and, since it was late, decided to turn in.

"Jacquie, meet my roommate, Fred."

CHAPTER 3

I woke up about eight the next morning. It was already starting to get hot, but that was a good thing—it was going to be a perfect day at the beach. My friend Leo Whalen had invited me and our friend Marco Rams down for the day and asked me to pass the invite on. He had an apartment in Manhattan Beach, a little beach town on Santa Monica Bay. It was a nice place, but smaller than mine and cost twice as much. Living at the beach would be nice, but I loved the roominess of my place, and I was much closer to work.

I called Marco. I had worked with both him and Leo in the mail room at the bank before I transferred to the Foreign Exchange Trading Department, and he was also my wheel man when I went out on the occasional repo. Both he and Leo still worked the swing shift in the mail room. I told him to meet me at Leo's for a day of surfing, and he happily agreed.

Since I would probably be home late, I made sure Fred had enough food and water to keep him going until I got home, then swung by Mom and Pop's to pick up Pop's '66 Bronco—he never seemed to mind me borrowing it without notice. My long board was stashed inside. I loaded it up with an ice chest full of Coronas, said hi to Mom and Pop, and headed out.

I arrived at Leo's place about ten. Marco was already there, taking his board off the roof of his gray VW bug. Honestly, SoCal denizens will attach surfboards to any ramshackle contraption that can get them to the beach. I was amazed that he could even fit into that little car, considering that he was about six feet, two inches tall and weighed about 350 pounds. He cut a very imposing figure. For his size, he was extremely agile, which made him an ideal backup, especially when I needed both muscle and agility.

Leo was just coming out of his house carrying his board down to join us. He was about an inch shorter than Marco, and about 150 pounds lighter. When standing next to each other, they looked like Laurel and Hardy. Leo was what you might call a hippie-surfer type. Whereas Marco had short, cropped hair and a neatly trimmed mustache and could pass for an FBI field agent, Leo perpetually wore a red bandanna to keep his shaggy locks in check. He also had a full bush on his upper lip. Think Sam Elliott in *Lifeguard*. By contrast, my hairstyle and mustache were somewhere in the middle—people sometimes tell me I look like Tom Selleck.

After unloading, we asked a passerby to take a group picture. There we were, the three musketeers, surfboards at our back, each with a bottle of beer in hand—affirming, naturally, that it was five o'clock somewhere—toasting our day at the beach. I was hoping Jacquie would be impressed when I showed her the picture and maybe be a little jealous that she couldn't have been there. But let's face it—I think it was me that was missing her, to even entertain such a silly thought.

As it was time to surf, we got our things together and grabbed our boards and the cooler of beer and headed for the beach.

The sky seemed bluer than usual, and the ocean looked uncharacteristically cold. But the waves were perfect. Best of all was the scenery—there were plenty of surfer girls in bikinis, even if none of them were as cute as Jacquie. It was right out of a beach party movie—the only people missing were Frankie and Annette. God, I loved California!

We laid out our blanket and towels, grabbed our boards, and headed into the waves. I managed to get up on the first wave and rode for a few feet before crashing headfirst into the surf. The rest of the day went pretty much the same way.

After about six hours, we were pretty toasted and not just from the sun—the cooler was empty. We headed back to Leo's living room and began drinking a resupply of Coronas from Leo's well-stocked fridge. Leo put some classic jazz on the stereo, and we were all kicking back chillin' with a little Brubeck, a cold brew, and a joint, when Leo's brother John arrived.

John was out here from Boston and staying with Leo for a month or two. With him were a couple of people he had met at Cap'n Pete's, a local beer joint. The new people included Ray Ricco, a piano-lounge entertainer from Vegas, and a leggy blonde named Debbie Long, an aspiring singer. Since they didn't have any place to stay, John, with Leo's blessing of course, had invited them to stay with him and Leo. At the time, it wasn't quite clear to me why Ray and Debbie were here in the first place, but who in their right mind could turn down a stay at a Southern California beach? So I stopped wondering about it.

Since Leo had an old upright piano sitting smack in the middle of the living room, it didn't take much to convince Ray and Debbie to give us a live performance. They weren't that bad.

After a couple of hours, we were out of beer again, so I volunteered to make a run. Debbie decided to go with me because she wanted some snacks—she also seemed like the restless sort, and I would soon find out to what extent. When we pulled back up in front of Leo's, she made a move on me: It was a deep-throat kind of kiss. Debbie was hot, but I had Jacquie, who was even hotter, back in my life and I didn't want to blow it for a one-night fling with Debbie, so I decided to pass. It was an easy choice.

"I thought you were with Ray," I said.

"I am," she said, "but he's not all that good in the sack and I thought it'd be nice to try something different."

"I'm flattered, but I already have a girlfriend—you know how it is," I said.

"Too bad," she said. "I'm pretty good."

"I'm sure you are," I replied, and with that, we went back inside.

While we were gone, one of Leo's neighbors had dropped by, as neighbors tend to do at the beach, and everyone was smoking a joint. I settled in with another cold one, took a hit, didn't inhale— ha ha—and enjoyed the party. The neighbor's name was Dirk. Debbie, with a major itch to scratch, it seemed, was hitting on Ray, who was ignoring her, so she turned her attention to Dirk— and it wasn't long before the two of them disappeared.

It also wasn't very long before Ray noticed. Ray was more than a little pissed, so he, Marco, Leo, and I headed over to Dirk's apartment to see if we could find them. After some serious door banging, and Ray's ill-fated attempt to smash through the door—knocking himself out in the process—the door was suddenly opened by Don, Dirk's roomie. It turned out that Dirk and Debbie weren't there after all, but Don decided to join our merry band of searchers.

We carried Ray back to Leo's for John to take care of and the rest of us headed down to the beach to see if we could find Dirk and Debbie. After an hour of wandering the beach with no luck, we headed back to Leo's for more beer.

When we got back, Ray was now awake. A few minutes later, a very sheepish Debbie strolled in followed by an equally sheepish Dirk. She went over to Ray who rebuffed her again, and she stormed out, only to return about an hour later. By the end of the evening, Ray had passed out again, Dirk and Don had gone home, and Debbie had wandered off with Leo. You needed a scorecard to keep track of all these people, but I guess in the end everybody was happy. Anyway, there was only John, Marco, and me left. We were running out of beer again, and with all the sun and beer, I was tired and decided to head home. I could sleep in on Sunday and be all rested up for work on Monday.

I found out later from Leo that, according to Debbie, Dirk was aptly named.

Hmmm.

Okay, so I said I love Southern California; I never said it was the height of social decorum! But much more to the point, little did I know, ironically enough, that a couple of these folks were going to figure in the caper that would commence on Monday night, when I embarked on my "mission" for Uncle Jack.

CHAPTER 4

Monday morning came way too early. I got up at my usual six o'clock and it was already approaching eighty-five degrees. It was going to be another hot one. I decided to leave the air conditioner on all day for Fred, though I really wasn't looking forward to my electric bill that month.

I showered, shaved, and got dressed. I grabbed a Coke out of the fridge—I'd never been big on coffee as my primary caffeine source—and headed out. I was sitting at my desk in the trading room by seven.

The L-shaped trading room stretched around the south and west sides of the building, with the FX trading section clustered in the southwest corner. Most of the desks in the trading room were plain, industrial-style steel and set up perpendicular to the windows, like a row of soldiers at attention. The FX desks were different; ours were made out of mahogany and were laid out in two sections. The inner section was a hexagonal shape topped by loads of computer screens and TV monitors. The TV monitors were the kind you'd find in any stock brokerage or, in this case, FX trading room—bulky, as deep as they were wide, and taking up a good portion of the desks they sat on. They allowed the traders to keep abreast of the market at all times. The computers—Olivetti Programma 101s—came out in 1965, and they were the first of their kind that could be considered a desktop.

The outer sections were sets of three desks facing inward on the four points of the compass. Mine was on the outer section facing south. That gave me a beautiful view of South Central LA through the window on the opposite wall. On a clear day, you could see Catalina. This was one of those days. I wasn't really thinking about my caper that evening; I was too caught up in thinking about Catalina and sailing. Yeah, I kinda did that a lot whenever I was sitting at my desk in the office. FX trading isn't as exciting as you might expect.

I had had lunch that Sunday with Jacquie, despite my throbbing head, and I had talked her into giving me a photo of herself. It was a professionally posed portrait, and she was wearing a lovely purple knit turtleneck top, formfitting in a way that accentuated her curves. She was absolutely beautiful and reminded me of the actress Jill St. John. Only prettier, if you'll forgive my bias. I was putting the photo on my phone board when Kathy walked up. Since I'd already asked Jacquie to go sailing, I decided to invite Kathy and her husband Ron to join us—this would be a great way to introduce them to each other. Kathy and Ron were easygoing and fun, and I envisioned us having a good time together. Also, they had both been sailing before and I could certainly use the help.

But before I could ask, she blurted out, "Um . . . where did you get that picture of my friend Jacquie?"

"What?" I asked incredulously. Then it came together. "You mean to tell me that the Jacquie in this photo, whom I've known since her parents moved in next to mine out in La Quinta, the same Jacquie who is now my dad's office manager and hopefully my future girlfriend, is the same Jacquie that you have been carrying on endlessly about how wonderful she is, only to refuse to show me her picture or set me up with her as I've been asking you to? *That* same Jacquie?" I sounded like a DA in court, coldly identifying the perp in front of the jury.

"Eh . . . yes?" she said. "Sorry?"

"Wow," was all I could say.

For several moments we just stared at each other in eye-blinking silence, listening to all the background activity in the trading room. It took a few seconds to sink in.

"Wow," I repeated, unable, for the moment, to process this phenomenon any further than that. When I regained my faculties, I said, "You owe me one, and what was the big deal anyway? Why couldn't you introduce us?"

"I don't know," she whined, "I guess I was afraid if I did and it didn't work out, you both would blame me."

I just laughed and said, "Well, considering how it turned out, that seems highly unlikely. What's important is that Jacquie and I managed to find each other again."

"You're right and I'm really happy for you," she said, apparently relieved.

"Cool," I said, quickly changing the focus. "Jacquie and I are going sailing this weekend, and I was going to ask if you and Ron would like to go along so I could introduce you to her. Obviously, introductions won't be necessary, but the invite's still open if you'd like to come along."

"We'll be there," she said gleefully. "We'd have gone along in any case, but now there is no way I would miss this."

"Cool," I repeated, as I turned to get back to work. I just shook my head and said "Wow" again. The phone was ringing, and it was time to settle in for the day's work.

———

After work, I went home and changed. I swung by Pop's and picked up the envelope that I was supposed to deliver and headed out. I couldn't get past the feeling that something about this didn't seem quite right. When somebody says, "Don't worry, there's nothing to it," that's usually the time to start worrying. Fat Albert probably thought this would be routine, but the more he reassured me that it was a cakewalk, the more uneasy I felt. *Always listen to your gut* is a thing for a reason. Seriously, it's never wrong. So, I did my due diligence and got out my .38 Colt diamondback revolver and made sure it was loaded. I grabbed some extra rounds and strapped those to my belt. You know what they say: It's better to have it and not need it than to need it and not have it.

It's great advice, trust me. Feeling I was about as prepared as I could be, I just shrugged and headed out the door.

I arrived at the address about a half hour before the meetup was scheduled. The place overlooked downtown LA. The sun was setting, a big red orb shining through the smoggy haze. I looked out at it, thinking, *I can't believe we actually breathe that shit.* It was beautiful though, with the sun glinting off the glass of the skyscrapers like gold and copper—the City of Angels.

I went up and tried the front door. Locked. I knocked and got no answer. So, I decided to wander around the house. I got around to the back balcony; the place had an even better view from back there. Too bad I couldn't take the time to enjoy it. The sliding glass door was open. Either Mr. Ricotta was a lousy housekeeper, or the place had been tossed. Stepping quietly inside, I surmised this was obviously not a burglary; stuff was in disarray all over the place, but the stereo, TV, and everything else that appeared to have any value were still there. At that moment I heard what sounded like heavy breathing coming from the front of the house. I knew I was going to need my gun. I pulled my .38 and slowly approached the room where the sound appeared to be coming from. Just then four shots rang out. Lucky for me, the shooter missed. Just as I came around the corner, there was a loud thud, more heavy breathing, then nothing.

There on the floor lay my shooter, dead.

He had two slugs in him, his lifeless body crumpled on the floor like yesterday's trash. Clutched in his dead hand was a 9mm automatic and it was still warm. I hate to say it, but he fit perfectly into the décor of the tossed apartment. Just then I heard footsteps running out the back.

I made a dash out onto the balcony, but whoever it was, was gone. I went back inside and noticed two bullets lodged in the door opposite the vic, confirming, at least for the moment, that I had indeed heard four shots. I was sure that someone else—anyone remotely nearby—had to have heard them, so I had to work fast. I grabbed a handkerchief out of my hip pocket and carefully pulled his wallet.

My shooter-turned-victim was a Lester Sloan. I looked at the address and recognized it, as I'd been there before. I remembered that it was a run-down flophouse over on Franklin in Hollywood that would be my next stop after I finished here. It was looking like the shots weren't meant for me after all.

Now I heard sirens coming from down in the valley below. It wouldn't be long before the cops got there, and I decided I didn't want to hang around. I made a mental note of Lester's address, put his wallet back, and got the hell out of there.

I had just gotten in my car and was rolling slowly down the

hill when the cops arrived. They were focused on the crime scene and paid no attention to me as I snuck away. I decided to head to Hollywood.

Kit searches for clues.

CHAPTER 5

I had a lot to think about on my trip to Hollywood. Lester obviously wasn't R. Ricotta. And who in the hell was the other shooter? Was that Ricotta? I hoped I'd get some answers at Lester's pad.

The trip took about a half hour. I parked in the Ralph's Supermarket parking lot across the street from Lester's building. It was your standard '50s-era apartment building. You had to be buzzed in. I punched all the buttons. Finally, the entry door clicked, and I was in, no questions asked. I found Lester's apartment down in the basement level. *So predictable*, I mused. I tried his door, and it gave on the first nudge, so I let myself in.

Lester's place was a mess too—only this time I think that was just the way he lived. The last place I saw him—his lifeless carcass, that is—that place had been ransacked. But no one had tossed this place, so he really didn't have any excuses for this mess. I started as methodical a search as was possible under the circumstances. When you're confronted with this kind of chaos, you have to possess a kind of intuitive radar to sense something important or relevant among the piles of overdue bills and the empty white containers from Chinese takeout. I was searching the bathroom, which was rank with the smell of cheap disinfectant, and I soon discovered why Lester was such a heavy breather. The medicine cabinet was full of asthma medicine and heart pills. If the bullets hadn't killed him, his flagging health probably would have doomed him sooner rather than later.

I continued searching the bathroom. Suddenly, I found an item that looked like it might be something significant. There, stuffed behind some old magazines in a rack on the wall, was a worn manila envelope containing a bunch of old newspaper clippings cut from a Vegas newspaper from the '50s. I sat down on the closed toilet seat and began to sift through.

Most of the clippings were about the death of the infamous gambler Tony Cornero. It was a story many of us knew—back in the day, Tony ran a fleet of gambling ships off the coast in Santa Monica Bay. The flagship was the *SS Rex*. Although calling it a "flagship" was quite a stretch. From the pictures in the papers, one could surmise that the *Rex* was only slightly larger than the Catalina ferry, and it looked like a shabby two-story Route 66 roadside motel that had somehow been put to sea, sitting precariously low in the water.

In any case, after his ships were closed down in the early '40s, he moved his operations to Las Vegas and opened one of the first legal casinos in that town. One night in July of 1955, Tony was down ten Gs in an all-night craps game. Desperate and determined to turn his fortunes around, Tony stood up tall, blew on the dice, and tossed them on the table, whereupon he immediately dropped dead from a massive heart attack. At least, that was what was reported as the official cause of death. Some, however, thought he was murdered.

I found another article about a different death that had occurred that same year. The mistress of a gambler by the name of Nick Colleti was killed in an automobile collision. The article also suggested at the time that it might not have been an accident. The byline on both articles was none other than Lester Sloan.

I heard noise coming from the living room and quickly put the envelope back where I'd found it. I flushed the toilet and walked out into the living room, where I found myself confronted by two LAPD detectives from the Hollywood Division. I knew they were cops by their appearance. I'd seen it many times. Short, well-groomed hair, big and tough physiques. They were wearing standard rumpled suits that looked like they had been wearing them for a week and they looked tired, like it had been a long shift, even though it had probably just started. They were standing just inside the door, surveying the seedy premises, and I think they were startled by my sudden appearance.

The one who looked like he was in charge flashed his badge and said he was Detective Sergeant Malloy. "Who are you and what are you doing here?" he asked brusquely.

"I'm a private investigator," I responded quickly. "Mr. Sloan asked me to meet him here about some possible work," I said. "The door was open, so I came in to look for him. I needed to use the john, so I helped myself. That's when you came in."

"Are you carrying?" Malloy asked.

"Yes, I am," I said. I still had my .38 strapped to my belt.

"Hand it over very carefully," said the other cop, who had identified himself as Detective Johnson.

I kept my hands visible and lifted my jacket. I faced him, leaning in so he could pick up the gun himself.

While Johnson took my gun, Malloy asked, "Do you have a license for that?"

"Yes," I said, "that and my PI license are in my wallet. Can I reach for them?"

"Yes, but very slowly," he said.

I pulled my wallet out with two fingers—it wasn't easy—and handed it to Johnson.

"He's legit," Johnson said, after fishing through my wallet and finding what he needed.

"Still, I think you need to accompany us to the station," Malloy said. "I think the captain would like to have a word with you."

"Okay," I said as I held out my wrists to be cuffed.

"That won't be necessary for right now," Malloy said. "You're not under arrest yet."

Typical. If they arrested me, they'd have to read me my rights. This way they could go on a little fishing expedition.

CHAPTER 6

When we arrived at the station at about nine o'clock, Johnson took me to an interrogation room while his partner went looking for their captain. It was about an eight- by ten-foot space, and the one door was the only way in or out. There were two-way mirrors on the wall next to the door so the subject in interrogation could be observed from the outside. A drab metal table in the center of the room was bolted to the floor and around it were four metal chairs, two on each side of the table. On the table was what looked like a chain link firmly bolted, so the subject could be cuffed to it if necessary.

I asked, "Can I have my one phone call, you know, just in case?"

"Go ahead, smart ass," Johnson said. "The pay phone is in the hall."

I popped my dime in the phone and called my parents' house. Mom answered.

"Hi, Mom," I said. "I need to speak to Pop right now. It's kind of important."

"Just a minute," she said. I heard her yell off somewhere in the background, "Frenchy, it's Kit on the phone. He needs to talk to you—says it's urgent."

A few moments later, Pop picked up.

"Yeah, Bud, what's up?" he asked.

"Our little caper that was supposed to be a cakewalk went south," I told him. "I'm with the cops at the Hollywood station. I haven't been arrested yet, but you might want to get Fat Albert over here right away and maybe even Carl G. I may need them both."

"I'll get on it," he said and hung up without another word.

Carl G. was Carl G. Moberg, our bail bondsman. He would send his partner Bud Poole over to bond me out if worse came to worst.

After my call, I was escorted back to the interrogation room where I waited and I waited. Finally, the two detectives came in with another cop. This one looked like he might be in charge. He introduced himself as Captain Wallace.

"You're Frenchy O'Banion's kid, aren't you?" he asked.

Hollywood Division was where my old man worked out of before he retired and went private. There were still a lot of cops around who knew him, or knew of him and his rep. He was known as a good, if somewhat unorthodox, detective. He often walked the line between what he was and wasn't supposed to do, and occasionally stepped over a bit.

"Yes," I said. "Am I under arrest?"

"No," he said, "but I do have a couple of questions for you."

"Shoot," I said.

"Funny choice of words," he said. "So, how well did you know Lester Sloan?"

"As I told the other two detectives, he called our agency and said he wanted to hire us to do a little research for something he was working on. I was supposed to meet him at his apartment to find out what he wanted. When I knocked, the door was open, so I let myself in to see if he was home. That's when your two detectives arrived."

"How did you get past the security door?" he asked.

"I went in as someone else was leaving," I lied.

"Did you know that Lester Sloan was dead?" he asked.

Giving an Oscar-winning performance, I shook my head somberly. "I didn't know that—if I had, I wouldn't have wasted my time going to his apartment, would I? When and how?"

"Shot twice," he said. "About an hour before my detectives picked you up at Sloan's apartment."

"Am I a suspect?" I asked.

"Not for now. You were, but your gun didn't appear to be fired. In fact, it smelled as if it had recently been cleaned. When was the last time you cleaned it?" he asked.

"This morning," I said.

"How convenient," he responded. "We tested your gun anyway and we'll compare it to whatever we pull out of our victim. Just in case."

"Just in case of what?" I said. "Where did you say he was killed?"

"Actually, I didn't say. But I think I can tell you now that it was at a house up on Mt. Washington," Wallace said. "Why do you ask?

"You guys are rich," I said "You tested my gun just in case I shot Lester up on Mt. Washington, cleaned my gun, and got all the way over to Hollywood, broke into his apartment, just so you could find me there? I'm not that fast or that stupid. Gimme a break."

"You're as big a smart-ass as your old man," he said. "Get out of here before I change my mind. You won't be needing the lawyer or the bond agent you got waiting for you out in the lobby."

"I take it I'm free to go?" I asked.

"Get outta here," he growled. "We know how to find you if we need you."

"Can I bum a lift back to my car?" I asked, just for the fun of being annoying.

"Get out!" he yelled.

"I'll take that as a no. Well, goodbye and thanks for the use of the room," I sneered as I hustled out of the interrogation cell.

I got my gun and wallet from the booking clerk and found Fat Al and Bud Poole in the lobby. I told Fat Al to arrange a meeting in Pop's office for tomorrow afternoon.

"I'm too tired to go through everything now. Just have Uncle Jack and yourself in Pop's office right around two. I'll explain then," I said.

Fat Al agreed and left. I bummed a ride to my car off Bud Poole. It was still parked at the Ralph's across from Lester's apartment—it was the only one left in the parking lot. This thing had eaten up my whole afternoon and evening, but I still had one more thing to do before I could call it a night. It was also convenient that Bud had driven me—Bud usually carried, and I could use the backup for what I had to do.

I asked if he could stay a few and help me out and he said he was happy to do so.

I looked across the street and scoped out Lester's apartment building, and as far as I could see in the dark, there appeared to be no cops lingering around, no crime scene tape . . . nothing to indicate that anything out of the ordinary had happened there earlier that evening.

As I popped the trunk of my car to get my flashlight and two Boy Scout Walkie Talkies, I said to Bud, "Take this Walkie Talkie and cover me. I'm going to get back into Lester's apartment and get that package I hid from the cops. If you see anything suspicious, especially more cops, give me a heads-up so I can get the hell outta there."

"No problem, I got your back," Bud said.

It was too late to start buzzing doorbells, so I had to find another way into the building. As said, I'd been there previously on another case. I had to sneak in that time too. I remembered that I had gotten in through a transom window with a broken latch, which dropped into the dank hallway that led to the basement row of apartments. The very floor that Lester's apartment was on.

As silently as I could, I worked my way around to the side of the building. I got lucky. Just as I remembered it, there, hidden behind some bushes next to the sidewalk that led to the back from the street, was the window I'd used before, and the latch was still broken.

The hallway had no lighting other than the moonlight that reflected off the cheap black-and-white tile floor, and a spooky red "EXIT" sign that flared above the steel fire door at the far end of the corridor. There had been no one in the street as I approached, and as far as I could tell, there was no one in the alley behind the building. I checked it out anyway just to make sure. Yup— just trash cans, some lying on their sides with the putrid garbage spewing out on the ground, and a couple of parked cars. The place smelled of chicken bones, and the only movement was a stray cat chasing a rat behind the trash cans. I eased myself through the transom. A few late-night TV shows resonated from some of the other apartments, eerie blue light emanating from beneath the doors, but for the most part it was quiet. So far so good—it seemed that no one had heard me.

I made my way down the hall to Lester's door. The cops were getting sloppy—Lester's door was still ajar. Or maybe Lester's door lock just didn't work so good. Whatever the case, as quietly as I could, I made my way back to the bathroom. If my luck held, the manila envelope would still be where I left it. It was. I grabbed it and got the hell out of there.

When I got back to our cars, Bud asked, "How did it go? There was nothing happening out here that I could see."

"Piece of cake," I said as I waved the envelope at him. "In and out in a flash—no fuss, no muss."

"Yeah, just like you knew what you were doing," he said with a laugh.

"Copy that," I said. "We're done here. Thanks for everything. Get on home to your lovely wife and kiss her for me."

"No problem. I'm glad I could help," he said. "Besides, I'm sure Carl G. will be sending your old man a bill."

"Oh, I'm sure we can count on that!" I said.

We both laughed and said goodnight.

By the time I got home and hit the sheets, it was 4:15 a.m., and there was no way in hell I was going to get up in an hour and forty-five minutes and get ready for work. My alarm went off at six as usual. I called in sick and went back to sleep.

I finally woke up around noon. After I showered and shaved, I called Kathy at work to see if I'd missed anything important, or if anybody had said anything about me calling in sick. Nobody had, and the only tidbit of news was that Suzy Jones, the position clerk from our London office, was coming over for cross training. She would be here Friday afternoon. I was in London myself for cross training about a month earlier, for a couple of weeks. They'd hired Suzy the day I left, so I never really got a chance to meet her. I didn't know much about her, but an idea came to mind.

I said to Kathy, "I have an idea. Why don't you invite her along on Saturday, then we can write the day off with the bank for entertaining a visiting fireman."

"I'll mention it to her when I talk to her later to make arrangements to pick her up at the airport," she said.

Great. The bank was going to pay for our day's sailing. At least for the food and drink. I got into some comfortable clothes and headed over to Pop's office.

CHAPTER 7

I arrived at Pop's office about a half hour before Uncle Jack and Fat Albert. After giving Jacquie a little kiss, I went through the rec room and grabbed a couple of cold ones on the way into Pop's office, where I briefly filled Pop in on the previous evening's events.

"Wow," he said, "Jack has some explaining to do."

"No shit," I said. "I'm pissed."

"No kidding," Pop said, with a bit of levity in his voice.

Fat Albert and Uncle Jack arrived first, and Max, who had been parking Jack's car, followed shortly thereafter; they could see that I was just a little angry.

While everyone was getting situated around Pop's desk, Max pulled me aside and said, "Hey, I hear things got a little rough last night. You okay?"

"Yeah? What makes you say that?" I asked sarcastically. "There was just the usual, you know, people shooting at each other, a dead body with two slugs in him, a trip down to the station house to meet some nice policemen," I said. Much as I was trying to lighten the mood, I wasn't hiding my anger.

"Did you see who was doing the shooting?" he asked.

"Nope, whoever it was got away clean," I told him.

"Well, at least you're all right," he said with smile as he patted me on the back. "If you ever need backup, you know you can always call me. Seriously."

"Yeah, thanks," I said and shook his hand.

Then Fat Al called the meeting to order and the first words out of his mouth were, "I can explain everything. But first, tell us what the hell happened at the drop."

"To make a long story short," I said, "Lester Sloan started shooting at me, and then someone shot him. There was no R. Ricotta around. I have no clue who the shooter was. My first guess is that it could be R. Ricotta who shot Lester Sloan, or maybe Sloan was using the alias R. Ricotta, and the shooter was someone else entirely. Right now, I'm not sure of anything. The only thing I have that might provide a clue is this manila envelope with a bunch of old newspaper clippings in it."

I showed them to Uncle Jack and Fat Albert, and said, "I found these at Sloan's apartment; they mean anything to either of you?"

Fat Albert sat grimly silent for a moment, then finally spoke. "I said I could explain."

"No," Uncle Jack interrupted. "Let me."

He continued, "Back in the day, Tony Cornero, Nick Colleti, and I were partners. The association went all the way back to the SS Rex, and it continued into the years and the casinos in Vegas. The night Tony died, he'd had an argument with Nick. Nick had threatened to kill Tony. Nick and I also had something else in common: Ruth Roman, a lounge singer."

"The one mentioned in some of these articles?" I asked.

"The one and the same. After she and I broke up, she became

Nick's squeeze. She witnessed the argument between Tony and Nick, and when Tony ended up dead under questionable circumstances, she got scared and asked me to help her disappear. With the help of a couple of cops that were on Tony's and my payroll, Max and I faked a traffic accident and Ruthie was relocated to New York, where she later got married."

I looked at Max quizzically.

"I remember it like it was yesterday," Max said. "I'm glad we did it. I really liked Ruthie—she was a class act."

While Uncle Jack was collecting his thoughts, Pop asked, "But how does Lester Sloan fit in to all of this?"

"I'm getting to that," Jack said. "Lester was a reporter for the local paper at the time, and always suspected that Nick actually did kill Tony and that he was responsible for the death of Ruthie—although he never had anything concrete he could take to the authorities. This is all old news, from back in the '50s and early '60s when those articles were published. To tell you the truth, I never thought I'd ever be talking about all this again.

"But then, about a month ago, this guy calling himself R. Ricotta calls me and demands ten thousand dollars or he'll go to Nick and tell him Ruthie is alive, gone into hiding. I assumed it was Lester Sloan and agreed to the meet. That's where you came in. Maybe there's an R. Ricotta, maybe not, and maybe he killed Lester Sloan, or maybe not. Until we have more information, I think we have to assume there is a character out there identifying himself as R. Ricotta and that he is our shooter. But we have his evidence now, so unless we hear from Ricotta, this is probably over."

"Well," I said, "if Lester and Ricotta are the same person, then we have another shooter. But I think it's safe to assume that Lester and Ricotta are two separate people and Ricotta is still at large and probably dangerous. But I have to disagree with you about one thing, Jack. I'd be willing to bet we'll hear from him again. And probably sooner rather than later is what I'd put my money on."

"I still have friends over at Hollywood Division," Pop said. "There's been a murder and they're not going to drop this. I'll keep tabs on their progress with my contacts there."

Then Fat Albert spoke up. "We'll deal with this Ricotta, if and when he contacts us again. Your father will keep us in the loop regarding the police investigation. In the meantime, as I told you before, all of this is privileged information. You don't need to tell the police anything if you're called in for questioning again. Your father and I will make sure our story jibes with yours when—that is, if—the police call to verify it."

"We'll see," I said, "especially since I've already lied to the cops about my relationship to Lester Sloan."

"Don't worry," Pop said. "That's why Al gets the big bucks. We've got it all under control."

"Uh huh, and this money drop was supposed to be a walk in the park. I'll believe it when I see it," I said with a smirk.

"Copy that," Pop said, smiling.

Everyone laughed.

"Not to worry," Fat Albert said. "I've got this. I think we're done here. You can go now—I need to talk to Jack and your father alone, if you don't mind."

"Okay, works for me. Catch you on the flip side," I said as I rose, thinking about how the ending of this meeting—that is, my part of it again—was so strikingly similar to the ending of the previous one that had initiated this whole fiasco. This time I couldn't help but wonder what they *weren't* telling me.

Fat Albert, Jack, Max, and Pop all got up and we shook hands. I headed out into the anteroom to see Jacquie and they all resumed their seats to talk.

CHAPTER 8

The rest of the week was uneventful. I had dinner with Jacquie once more, and that was the highlight of my week. We were both looking forward to our sailing outing. I was particularly looking forward to it because it would also kick off the start of an overdue weeklong vacation that I'd been anxiously anticipating for the last six months. Kathy and Ron were definitely coming, especially now that Kathy knew my Jacquie and hers were one and the same. And since we had Suzy from London going along as well so the bank would pick up the tab, it was virtually guaranteed to be a good time. Nothing I like better than spending leisure time on the company dime!

I didn't tell Jacquie about the surprise in store for her. I could hardly wait to see the look on her face when she saw Kathy. I had asked Kathy to play along and stay quiet, and she said she was happy to.

Friday night, after work, I left the Mustang at my parents' and borrowed the Bronco again. I had way too much stuff to take to the boat to fit in my car. On Saturday morning, I picked up Jacquie at her apartment on Riverside Drive across from the riding stables, and we headed for Fleitz Brothers Marina, a funky and eclectic place down in San Pedro that Pop had always liked better than the more upscale Marina Del Rey. I liked it too. The bar at the main entrance wasn't bad, and there was a great restaurant—nothing fancy, but the seafood was fantastic. Especially the fried oysters and shrimp. It was the kind of place where they fried everything, including the french fries, with the skin on, in the same oil. Tasted great. Plus, they had a homemade hot sauce that was heavy on the black pepper, kind of Cajun style. Out of this world.

As I said before, my dad's boat, the *Black Widow*, was an old forty-foot wooden sloop he had built himself back in the 1920s. After he transferred to the LAPD, he had to find a new home for his boat. He took a liking to Fleitz Brothers Marina and had been there ever since. Having found a new home for the old girl, he resumed lobster fishing and continued right up to the start of the war, when he was ordered to take his boat out of the water for coming in too close to shore. They didn't want him dropping off any Japanese spies.

Now the boat was strictly used for recreational purposes, but he still preferred the old "workingman's marina," as he liked to call it.

"Oh, look," I said to Jacquie as we pulled in. "We've arrived on time, at about ten hundred hours. Like the nautical touch?"

Jacquie rolled her eyes good-naturedly.

We loaded all the goodies on board, stopped in the bait shop for a few things that Jacquie wanted, sunscreen, lip balm, etcetera, and waited for our three other guests. They arrived about a half hour later. Jacquie was totally taken by surprise all right—you should have seen the look on her face when her good friend Kathy, accompanied by Ron and Suzy, approached the boat. She gave Kathy a WTF look, then she turned and gave me that same look.

Then it hit her, and she said to Kathy while pointing at me, "Is he the guy that you've been telling me about?"

"Yes," she said, sheepishly.

"Wow," Jacquie said, then turned to me and asked, "Did you know about this?"

"Not until Monday when I was putting your picture on my phone board. It was as much of a shock to me as it obviously is to you. She's been talking about you for a long time, but I could never convince her to introduce us. Can you believe this?"

"Why didn't you tell me when you found out?" Jacquie demanded.

"Believe me, it was all I could do to *not* tell you, but I didn't want to spoil the surprise. Judging by your reaction, I think it was the right move," I said with a smile.

"Oh boy, both of you are going to get it," she said, teasingly. "I don't know how or when, but I will get you both back."

"I can hardly wait," I said as everybody started to chuckle, even her.

This junket really was going to be fun; I was now certain.

After we got all of their stuff on board and made last minute pit stops, we untied the old girl and backed her out of her slip. We motored out to the open part of the bay, hoisted sails, and headed out beyond the breakwater for some real sailing. Both Kathy and Ron had been out before, so they knew how to set the sails. Jacquie and Suzy hadn't, so they just did their best to stay out of the way, taking in the sun and the crisp salt air.

Once at sea, drinks in our hands and relaxing, we sat around enjoying the stunning brilliance of the sea and our drinks. We started to get to know each other better. Seeing Jacquie and Suzy sitting next to each other, I couldn't help noticing a remarkable resemblance. Suzy was older than Jacquie by about six years, but other than that they could pass for sisters.

"Suzy," I said, "now that we can relax, I'd like to introduce you to Jacquie."

The two women exchanged nods and smiles.

"Like you," I went on, "she's new in town. I've known her since we were kids. Her family has a place next to my family down in La Quinta. My dad just hired her to be his new office manager. As you may have gathered, she and Kathy are old friends too; Jacquie was maid of honor at Kathy and Ron's wedding.

"So at the office these past few months, Kathy's been talking about this mysterious friend of hers, who'd be perfect for me, she kept saying. But every time I asked her to introduce me, she'd just say 'No, I don't want to play matchmaker.' Funny how things have a way of working out."

"Yep, she's been doing the same thing to me. 'I know this really great guy at work, you'd really like him.' Yet every time I'd ask her to set something up, she'd just give me the same response as she gave Kit," Jacquie said.

Everybody laughed.

"How long have you been with the bank?" I asked Suzy.

"About a year. I transferred into the Foreign Exchange Department about six months ago," she replied in her British accent. That fit the timeline, as she came into the office on my last day of cross training.

I love British accents. The first British girl I ever fell in love with was Miss Moneypenny from the *James Bond* movies. If I weren't already falling for Jacquie, I might have gone for Suzy myself. Then I asked her about her family.

She said, "My father and mother met during the war. They were both in the British Navy. He was killed in action just before I was born, so I never knew him. My mother is still alive. She served as an attaché to the U.S. Naval Intelligence group stationed in London. She remarried after the war, and I was raised by her and my stepfather."

"What a coincidence," I said. "Both Jacquie's and my dad were in Naval Intelligence during the war and they too were stationed in London. That's really wild . . . Did your mom ever tell you about her experience and some of the people she served with? God knows, she might know our dads."

"No," she said. "My mom never told me much about her war-time experience. She never really seemed to want to talk about it."

Too bad, I thought to myself—maybe Pop or Jacquie's dad might remember her mom. I would have to ask when I saw them again.

The rest of the day was great. Well . . . except for one minor incident. I happened to be standing in the cockpit when Ron, who was steering, suddenly jibed, and the boom swung around, knocking me forward toward the lifeline. I managed to grab on in an attempt to break my fall. But instead of stopping the fall, I did a perfect somersault and went into the water feet first. I couldn't have made a better dive if I'd tried. The water was freezing. Fortunately, I had practiced man-overboard drills with Ron and Kathy, just in case something like this happened. Ron swung the boat around and eased up on me like a pro. They put the ladder over the side, and I climbed out of the drink.

Everyone was clapping and rating my dive. Ron gave me a five. Jacquie was more generous and gave me a ten. Suzy and Kathy both gave me a seven.

I just bowed and said, "Thank you, thank you very much," in my best Elvis impression. That only garnered more laughs.

Now I was soaking wet, and of course I hadn't brought a change of clothes. This was no laughing matter. I went below and rummaged around in the lockers. I managed to find some of Pop's clothes in there. Somebody has got to teach Pop how to dress. The only thing I could find was the most hideous pair of Bermuda shorts known to mankind and an ugly Hawaiian shirt that, if paired with the shorts, would make the words "that really clashes" a massive understatement. Ugh. In ordinary circumstances, I wouldn't have wanted to be caught dead in that outfit, but I had no choice. I grabbed a dry pair of deck shoes, dressed, and went topside. Kathy giggled and Jacquie—suppressing laughter—asked if she could have a picture with me, which I politely declined. After being righteously ridiculed for my ensemble, I sat down and grabbed another beer.

Hopefully my clothes would dry before we got back to the marina. I'd hate to go to dinner dressed like this. Fortunately, they did dry out. In spite of my dunking experience—and perhaps in part even because of it—everyone had a good time. Sun, wind, and beer had made for a tiring combination, so when we got back to our slip at the end of the day, all anybody wanted to do was adjourn to the fish restaurant.

"We will," I said, "but first we put the sails away and hose down the boat."

Everybody groaned.

"Quit your bitchin'," I said, trying to keep a straight face. "This is nobody's favorite part, but you always leave the boat the way you found it. That's just the rules. Besides, somebody has to do it and I'll be dammed if I'm going to do it by myself."

They all laughed, and Ron said, "Okay but the first round is on you."

"Copy that," I said.

Dinner was great. I splurged and had both fried oysters and oysters on the half shell. Jacquie, Suzy, Kathy, and Ron all had lobster—the one item on the menu listed at "market price" instead of an actual figure. Then we all headed home. Since this was technically my third date with Jacquie, I was hoping for more than a goodnight kiss when I got her home. No such luck, however—her mom was there babysitting Nick, and there wasn't anything I could do about it.

"Oh well. Better luck next time," she said as we stood saying goodnight at the door.

"You could send her home," I whispered with a smile.

"Sorry, not tonight. Both she and Nick are asleep, and I don't want to wake them up. Next time," she said as she kissed me again, a longer, lingering kiss that felt like it ran down my spine.

Rats. Not what I was hoping for but very promising. One more for the road and I was gone.

When I got home, ready to crash hard after the long day, my luck ran out yet again—there was a frantic message from Leo on my machine.

"Hey. Call me and come down here as soon as you get this. I think Ray and Debbie are in danger, and I've been threatened."

What was all this about? I called and left him a message then, tired as I was, headed down to Manhattan Beach.

CHAPTER 9

When I arrived, Leo's apartment had been tossed—and I mean seriously tossed. He had an impressive black eye and a bloody lip. John, Ray, and Debbie were nowhere to be seen.

"What the fuck happened?" I asked.

"Two guys burst in here this afternoon and told me that Ray and Debbie owed their boss in Vegas ten thousand dollars. If they didn't pay, they would kill them, and if they couldn't find them, they'd take it out on me," he said.

"Did you call the police?" I asked.

"No, they took John with them as a hostage and told me if I knew what was good for me—and for my brother—I wouldn't call the cops," he said. "You have to find Ray and Debbie, ASAP."

"Well," I said, "the good news is that I'm off tomorrow for vacation. The bad news is, now I have to spend it looking for two people I barely know, and I haven't a clue where to start."

"Me either, to be honest." Leo stood scratching his head, looking entirely useless.

"When was the last time you saw them? What were they wearing, and where were they headed?" I asked. It was time to get serious, and I was hoping we weren't too late.

"I saw them early this morning. They left in Ray's VW. I didn't pay any attention to what they were wearing—just jeans and T-shirts, I think. Wait a minute," Leo suddenly recalled. "They said something about heading out toward Palm Springs to see a guy named Spike at a bar called Sid's Lounge," he said.

"Did you happen to mention that to your big ugly friends?" I asked.

"Uh, I dunno. Maybe."

"There's no maybe,'" I told him. "Either you did or you didn't."

"Okay, I did." Leo turned pink and looked down at the floor.

"Well, maybe we can find this Spike before your new friends do," I said. "I've got to bring Pop in on this. Maybe he can get some DMV info on them and the van. In the meantime, lock this place up and come with me. You'll probably be safer with me at my place. At least I have a gun."

"Sure, yeah. Lemme just grab a couple things."

"You didn't happen to notice what kind of car your new friends were driving?" I asked, making no effort to keep the sarcasm from my voice.

"Yeah, wise guy," he responded in kind. "I did, okay? It was a late model Dodge Dart, light blue in color. I didn't catch the license plate, but I'd recognize it anywhere. It looked like it needed some bodywork."

"That's good," I said, smiling. "Now you're acting like a detective. Maybe we'll be able to spot them before there's trouble."

While Leo packed up a few things to take back to my place, I called Pop to fill him in on the caper—he wasn't going to like this.

He picked up on the first ring, sounding like I'd woken him up. "Hold on," he whispered into the handset. "Lemme go where I won't wake your mother."

I did appreciate the fact that he wasn't about to bring Mom in on all of this.

"This better be important to call at this hour," he said in an irritated voice when he came back on the line.

"Hi, Pop. Sorry to bother you so late, but something's come up and I need your help."

"What's up?" he asked in a somewhat less irritated tone. "You okay? You sound a little anxious."

"I'll give you the short version now. Some people I met—a guy and a gal—that were staying with my friend Leo are being chased by a couple of goons from Vegas. They're on their way to Palm Springs and the two goons have Leo's brother. Leo and I are going out to the Springs to see if we can find these folks—Ray something and Debbie something. I was hoping you could get a couple of people to stake out Leo's place down here in Manhattan Beach in case the goons show up again and to keep an eye out for John, just in case they turn him loose. I'll leave a photo under the doormat."

"Okay, got all that."

"Thanks, Pop. Also, I want to use the Hideaway as a base while we're down there. I know this is a lot to ask but—"

"No problem," he said. "It's been needing to be checked on real well in any case. I'll call Jack and have him go over and turn the air conditioner on for you—otherwise, it'll be hotter than hell in there—and I'll get a couple of our guys to watch Leo's place. It's a good thing you and Leo are friends and I like him."

"Copy that and thanks," I said. "I know this isn't a run-of-the-mill favor and I appreciate it, Pop."

I gave him Leo's address and a description of Ray, Debbie, and

John in case any of them showed up someplace before we were able to find them, and I also gave him descriptions of both Ray's VW and the blue Dodge Dart, asking him to see what he could get from the DMV.

"I probably won't be able to get that for you until Monday, but I'll see what I can do," he promised.

"Thanks again, Pop. Catch you later. Love you . . . and Mom— make sure and tell her," I said as I hung up.

We made a brief stop at the emergency room to take care of Leo's lip, which seemed to only be getting fatter and more split by the minute. It was good enough to get him a few days away from work. He'd have to call in sick from La Quinta on Monday. After gathering up a few things at my place, like my .38 diamondback and a 9mm, we gassed up the Bronco and headed for the desert.

It was almost three o'clock in the morning when we hit Palm Springs. Even though I knew it would be closed, I decided to swing by Sid's Lounge if for no other reason than to see where it was, and to scope the place out.

I gave Leo, who had fallen asleep, a little nudge. He only groaned.

"Wake up, sleeping beauty," I told him.

"Where are we?" he asked groggily. In the pre-dawn darkness and illuminated mostly by the faint dashboard lights, he was quite a sight with his black eye and fat lip.

"We-are-in-Palm-Springs," I said, enunciating each word in an effort to wake him up. "Even though it'll be closed, I thought we might swing by Sid's Lounge and see what there is to see. Sort of get the lay of the land, you know. I doubt if there will be anybody there, but stranger things have happened. Let's stop at that service station up ahead and see if they've got a phone booth. We can look up the address."

"Good idea," Leo acknowledged, still a little groggy.

Fortunately, the service station did have a phone booth. Even more fortunate, the phone book was mostly intact, hanging from the stainless-steel lanyard. We looked up the address and headed over. It was only a couple of blocks away. As I had expected, it was closed tighter than a drum. No activity and no cars—at least none that were recognizable—in sight, so we proceeded on to La Quinta.

We pulled into the carport at my parents' Hideaway a little after three o'clock.

It was a Southwest-style bungalow, with your typical desert landscaping. Pop had called ahead to Jack Judy, Jacquie's father, who looks after the place when Pop and Mom aren't there. The air conditioner had been turned on as promised so it was a comfortable seventy-five degrees inside even with it being in the nineties outside. We unloaded and settled in to get some sleep.

Pop would take care of things at Leo's place in Manhattan Beach, so I figured we would just head into the Springs in the morning and see if this Spike had made contact with Ray and Debbie or anyone else.

Lights out, I thought. Tomorrow's another day.

CHAPTER 10

When we finally woke up around ten, Leo and I headed over to the Cove, the beer bar owned by Jacquie's dad. It was tucked away on what passed for the main street in La Quinta and was small and dark, with intimate seating in its four booths and a handcrafted, cypress wood bar that ran all the way down one side. There was a small kitchen in the back room, where a bunch of well-used, dented, and scorched pots and pans hung cheerfully from the ceiling, and aromatic smoke from the ovens and grills spiraled relentlessly. Jack Judy was a fair to middlin' short-order cook, and the Cove was always open, seven days a week, or so it seemed.

"Hi, Jack," I said as we entered. "How's it going?"

"Not bad." He was in his usual place, shuttling between the bar and the kitchen.

"I'd like you to meet a friend of mine," I said. "This is Leo."

"Hi, Leo—a pleasure," Jack said as he came out from the kitchen, wiping his hands on his apron. Jack could not keep himself from squinting as he examined Leo's rearranged face, but he made no remark about it, choosing instead the discretion to let it lie.

"Jack and my dad are old Navy buddies," I said as they shook hands. "They met in London during the war—they'd both been assigned to Naval Intelligence. Pop because he was a cop and old Jack here was offered his pick of assignments after he was wounded at Pearl Harbor. They've been friends ever since. Oh . . . and that new girlfriend I told you about—that's Jack's daughter."

"Cool," Leo said.

"Your dad told me he was hiring Jacquie. And now I understand why," Jack said with an amused smile. "Welcome to the family."

I just grinned and said, "Thanks, *Dad*."

"We'll discuss all that later," he said, as we all laughed.

With everything that had happened since I met Suzy the day before, and in the course of our introductions, I totally forgot to ask Jack if he and Pop knew Suzy's mom. *I'll get to that later*, I thought, as Jack was already busy getting our breakfast together in the kitchen and I didn't want to bug him.

Breakfast was definitely the first order of business. Steak, hash browns, and eggs sunny-side up for me. Lots of homemade hot sauce—best described as "*WOW that's hot!*"—and a Coke. Leo had hot cakes, eggs over easy, and a cup of black coffee.

After breakfast, we headed over to Sid's Lounge. Even though it was early, dive bars like Sid's would typically be open by now, but it was still closed.

I parked the Bronco in a space where we could watch the front. I told Leo to stay put and keep an eye on the front while I poked around. I couldn't see any activity through the darkened front windows. The door was locked, so I went around to the alley behind to try the rear door. Lucky me—it was ajar. I gave it a little shove and presto, I was in.

There was very little room to maneuver in there—cases of beer and whiskey stacked high on both sides of the little pathway that led to the back entrance to the bar made for a narrow trail. The place also had its share of junk to trip over if you weren't careful, but I was lucky enough to get through without making a lot of noise.

Once in the bar area, I tried not to touch anything or leave any prints around. That proved to be a smart idea, as when I went behind the bar, there he was—Spike, slumped on the floor like he was asleep—right in front of the ice chest. He was still breathing and had only been knocked out. That was somewhat of a relief—we were clearly still in the realm of roughing people up and not killing them. But it was still looking very serious for Ray and Debbie if we didn't find them before Leo's visitors did.

After I let Leo in, I splashed Spike with soda water from the dispenser hose. As he slowly came to, I said, "What happened to you?"

Spike only groaned in response, putting a hand cautiously to his battered head.

"I'll bet I can guess," I said. "Two guys came in here looking for a guy and girl then beat the crap out of you when you couldn't or wouldn't give them any info. That about right?"

"Yeah. How did you know?"

"Been there, done that," I said. "So what did your two guys look like?"

"One was big as a barn and looked kinda dumb," Spike said. "He was all muscle. The other was shorter, and he ordered everybody around, especially the big guy, like he was the brains."

I looked at Leo. He nodded. It was the same two that had given him the black eye and fat lip. You could tell by the look on his face that he wanted payback.

"Have you heard from Ray?" I asked, as Spike managed to haul himself up off the floor.

"No, I haven't heard from him yet." He began to dig around in the ice and put together a pack, which he placed against the side of his balding head. "I think that may be the only reason they didn't kill me."

I thought he might be right. Since he had only been knocked out and was otherwise unhurt, there was no need to get the police involved. At least not yet. Besides, we wanted the place open in case Ray tried to make contact with Spike.

I went back to the car where Leo and I stayed in position for the next few hours in the hopes that Ray and Debbie might show up. Even having met Ray Ricco only briefly, I knew he was no dummy—he had some street smarts. He probably knew that sooner or later someone would be coming after him to collect the money he allegedly owed. Even if he didn't know they were hot on his tail, he would probably wait until it was dark to make contact and try, hopefully, to not be seen going in.

Eventually, we headed back to the Cove to regroup. I called Pop from there and gave him a summary of all the recent developments. He told me he'd managed to get the DMV info from a cop buddy and had faxed it to the machine that he kept at the Hideaway for business purposes.

Pop then said, "You can stop worrying about Leo's brother—what's his name . . . oh, yeah, John. He wandered into Leo's apartment early this morning. He told us—with no small amount of pride—that his captors decided he was more trouble than he was worth, so they got him drunk and left him in an alley to sleep it off. He said he woke up with a terrible headache, and just wandered his way home—claims he doesn't remember a thing. Our guys have got him safe—and they'll keep an eye on Leo's in case your friends come back, but I don't think that's likely."

"I agree. We'll lay low here for a few days and keep an eye on Sid's in case Ray and Debbie show up there. I'll keep you posted," I said.

"You better." Pop laughed. I appreciated him making the effort to keep things light.

We arrived back at Sid's just before dark and took up our positions. I took the front and Leo took up a position where he could watch the alley. We waited. And we waited. It was now pretty close to closing time. I had to pee, and I wanted a cold drink—a soda, a beer, anything. Still no sign of Ray or Debbie. Spike closed up, and we secretly followed him to his place.

There was no sign of our friends or Ray and Debbie there either. We gave it another hour and broke it off. We headed back to the house in La Quinta, where we found that Pop had left a message on the answering machine. A very brief message.

"New developments. Call me in the morning."

Now what, I wondered. But since there was nothing more we could do tonight, we had a beer and went to bed. Something told me I'd need my sleep more than ever.

CHAPTER 11

The following morning, after stopping for breakfast, I called Pop at the office.

"What's up?" I asked.

"We've heard from R. Ricotta again. He wants to set up another meet. He's going to call us tomorrow and let us know when and where."

"Good," I said. "That will give us another day to see if we can find Ray and Debbie before heading home."

"Sounds like a plan," Pop said.

"Keep me posted," I said.

"Will do," he said, and he hung up.

Leo and I hit the Springs about noon, just in time for the early lunch crowd. We pulled up in front of Sid's Lounge and found a parking spot. We saw the blue Dodge Dart parked in front of the place.

"Our friends are here," I said.

Leo looked around. "But I don't see Ray's VW, so hopefully, he and Debbie probably are not. Which is good."

"What do you want to bet our two friends are inside talking to Spike?" I asked.

"No bet," Leo said, shaking his head.

"Well, you're no fun," I said, and he laughed, though a little nervously.

I got out of the Bronco, went around, popped the hatch, and grabbed my little bag of goodies. I locked and loaded the 9mm and gave it to Leo.

"You do know how to use one of these?" I asked.

"Yes, I do—*duh*," he said and chuckled. "This ain't my first rodeo."

I loaded my .38 and stuffed it in my pants.

"I'll go around and come in the back. Let's sync our watches. Give me five—no, better make it ten—minutes. I may need to jimmy the door if it's locked. Then you come in with your gun drawn and make a lot of noise," I said.

"That I can do," Leo said.

I made my way around to the back and came in the same way I did the day before. Lucky for me the door wasn't locked today either. I made my way through the storeroom again, stepping over all the crap on the floor. I tried not to make any noise, but it wasn't easy. I looked through the barroom door. There wasn't much of a lunch crowd. Spike was behind the bar and seated in front of him were two guys. I assumed they were our friends from Manhattan Beach.

On cue, Leo came through the front door.

"Don't move! Keep your hands where I can see 'em!" he shouted. He sure was good at the noise thing. It was a great distraction.

I then took the opportunity to come in through the back.

"Make one wrong move and they'll be carrying you out of here feet first," I said.

I probably wouldn't shoot them, but they didn't know that. Sometimes it's fun being a badass. "Okay, boys, you know the drill," I said. "Hands on the bar and spread 'em. Spike, you pat 'em down and see what they're carrying."

The number one guy—the smarmy little brainiac of this sorry outfit—had a .38 special, a pair of brass knuckles, and a nine-inch switchblade knife. Number two—call him the Incredibly Dumb Hulk—had the same basic equipment, but he also had an ankle gun, a nice little .22 Derringer.

"My, oh my. Do your mothers know the kind of toys you're playing with?" I said, tsking at them for good measure.

Number one boldly said, "You leave my mom out of this."

"That's not what she said last night," I said, hoping to get a reaction.

It did. He made a move toward Leo, who promptly paid him back for the split lip with a smack across the jaw with the 9mm. The results were immediate . . . and impressive. A side of Leo I'd never seen before.

"That's for the other day," Leo said.

"Enough of the pleasantries," I said. "Sit in that booth over there in the corner so I can keep an eye on you. We need to have a chat."

The two men shuffled over and slid themselves into the high-backed booth. It was a tight squeeze for the Hulk. *Good*, I thought. That would make it a lot harder for him to try to lash his muscle out at anyone. The scrawny guy was one thing, but the Hulk appeared to be somebody who could do some real damage to Leo and me, given the right opportunity.

I got right down to business. "Talk! I want the truth! I find out you're fucking with me, it'll be the last time you fuck with anybody. Capiche?" With dramatic flair, I pointed my .38 right between his beady little eyes and demanded, "Speak!"

"Well, just like I told your friend here down at the beach, Ray owes my boss some money, and he wants to be paid," he said hesitantly. He looked at number two, who was grimacing. I pointed the .38 at number two and he squirmed in his too-tight seat.

"Okay, your turn," I said. "Let's hear your version, only I want the truth this time. Give."

He cleared his throat gruffly. "Yeah, like Vic here said, Ricco owes our boss some money. We followed them to a place in LA, then from there to a bar and dive shop in Manhattan Beach. Can you imagine that shit? It was a dive shop with a bar inside it! California is fuckin' crazy, ain't it, man?"

For all his size, I could see that the Hulk really didn't like being on the wrong side of a gun; he was actually nervous and starting to rant. I wanted him to get to the point.

"Never mind that," I ordered. "What did you do from there?"

"Well," the big lug continued, "we found out that they had gone off with that John guy, so we went over to his place to look for them. They were gone so we put the snatch on that John fellow and roughed up your friend as a warning. You know the rest," he said.

"So basically, you lost them? Remind me to never hire you mugs for a tail job. Your boss must really love your work. And here you are, just sitting around chewing the fat with ol' Spike here," I said, glaring at Spike. "Why do I get the feeling you haven't been totally honest with me, Spike? We'll have to discuss this further after I deal with these two."

I glared at number two again. "All right," I said, "a couple more questions. What's the name of your boss? I'm sure, at some point, we're going to have to talk about you two. I'm sure he's going to love your explanation about all this."

"Mo Weinstein," the Hulk volunteered.

I'd heard about Mo from my dad. He was a loan shark from Vegas, and not a guy you wanted to cross.

"Final question. What's the name of the bar you tracked them to?" I asked.

"Cap'n Pete's," the Hulk said.

That made sense. John liked to hang out there. I knew the place well. It was indeed a weird combination bar and dive shop, although there were dozens of them all up and down the Southern California coast. Captain Pete himself was an old friend of my Uncle Jack, and coincidentally enough, Pop and I had been renting our diving equipment there for years.

I checked their IDs. The big one was Frank Carpo, age thirty-eight—the short ugly one was Vic Steckler, also thirty-eight. Both of them were from Vegas.

"Where's the phone, Spike?"

Spike handed it to me from behind the bar and I dialed.

"Operator," the voice on the other end said.

"Police department, please. Non-emergency," I said. Spike just stood there staring at me.

A few minutes later, "Palm Springs Police Department," the pleasant voice said.

"Detectives, please," was my next request.

Another minute went by. "Detective squad, how may I help you?" the voice said.

"Is Lieutenant Armstrong on duty today?" I asked. There was a brief pause.

"Hey Rog, a call for you on 2," the guy yelled across the squad room.

Another minute. "Armstrong here—how may I help you?"

"Hi, Lieutenant. This is Kit O'Banion, Frenchy O'Banion's son," I told him. "How you doin' today?"

"Oh, just great," he said. "How's your old man? Haven't talked to him in a while."

"He's doin' great. I'll tell him you said hello when I see him. I'd like you to do him a solid if it's not too much trouble. He'd really appreciate it."

"I don't see why not," he said. "You workin' on something?" he asked.

"Yeah, I'll fill you in on the details when you get here. I've got a couple of fish I'd like you to put on ice for a week or two. We'll let you know when to kick 'em loose," I said.

"Can do. And you know how it is," Armstrong snickered. "Small town police department. Lose a lot of paperwork around here. We're gonna be computerized someday, so they say. Where you guys at?"

"We're at a dive over on North Palm Canyon called Sid's Lounge," I said.

"Know it well. Be there in twenty," he said as he hung up.

Spike was still staring at me, but it looked as though he'd begun to relax—I wasn't going to let him stay that way for long.

Armstrong was right on time. He had his partner Sergeant Dick Slade with him, and Armstrong's black 1969 Dodge Polara 440 was followed by a couple of prowlies in a Ford LTD black and white. After all the players were introduced, I filled the Lieutenant in on the details while Slade cuffed the boys and took their toys with them.

Slade took one look at the swag, let out a low whistle, and said, "This alone should be enough to keep these guys on ice for at least a couple of weeks while we sort this all out."

We exchanged knowing nods as he walked them out to the black and white. I smiled big at Frank and Vic as they were being escorted out.

"Well, bye for now, boys," I told them.

They didn't have much to say.

After they were gone, I turned my attention to Spike. As I grabbed him by his collar, I said, "Now it's your turn. Spill."

He started to stutter. "Ah, well, Ray and Debbie said they would check in today around four this afternoon."

"And you chose to tell Frank and Vic but not me," I said. "We need to work on our communication skills." It was now around two, and I was getting hungry. "This is a bar and grill, ain't it?" I asked.

"Ah, uh yeah," Spike stammered.

"Good," I said. "I'll have a double cheeseburger, rare, with grilled onions and fries."

"That sounds good," Leo said. "But make mine medium."

Spike went into the kitchen and started lunch. I grabbed some cold ones out of the fridge, and we made ourselves comfortable while we waited.

"Well, with Vic and Frank out of the picture for a little while, Ray and Debbie have some breathing room—at least until Mo finds out his two bozos have been taken out. Then he'll just send someone else. We need to find Ray and Debbie. They're not safe yet," I said.

The burgers arrived. Surprisingly enough, Spike wasn't a bad cook. The burgers were delicious. Finally, the clock struck four, and no phone call. I was just about to give Spike a dirty look when the door opened and two people walked in. It was none other than Ray and Debbie.

"Hi there. Remember us?" I said.

You could pretty much hear a pin drop as their jaws fell open.

"We need to talk, now," I said and offered them a seat in our booth.

When we were all seated, I looked at Ray and, in my best Ricky Ricardo imitation, I said, "Lucy, you have some 'splainin' to do." Then I got back to business. It was time to get tough. "I know it was none of my business when we first met, but it is now. Your friends from Vegas made it my business when they barged into Leo's looking for you. Notice Leo's fat lip and black eye. You see that?"

"Yeah, we see it," Ray grumbled as Debbie nodded.

"Well, it's Leo's business now too. We managed to put them on ice for now, but you owe Mo Weinstein big bucks, Ray, and he's just going to keep sending people after you until you pay up. So what do you plan to do? I hope you got some bright ideas."

Ray sat there mute, brooding.

"Also, there's Debbie here to think about," I added, piling on the guilt. "If you care for her at all, she's in danger too as long as she's hanging out with a loser like you."

"I'm going to pay him back," Ray squealed pathetically. "I just need to buy a little time. Spike here owes me a little money—I was going to give it to Mo, you know, like a deposit, and see if he'll give me a little extension for the rest."

"Fat chance," I said. "As soon as he finds out that Steckler and Carpo are off the board, he'll be sending someone else. The local cops are going to do my old man a favor and keep Laurel and Hardy on ice for a few days. That will give him and me a chance to plan our next move. Thanks to you, he's involved now too, whether he likes it or not. It's a good thing for you that he likes Leo."

Leo nodded somberly. "Sure is," he said.

"I figure we can hide you two out at one of our safehouses until we decide what to do about Mo Weinstein," I said. "By the way, since you've made it our business, how did you get on the hook for ten Gs to Mo, and just exactly how are you planning to pay him back?" I asked.

"That's why Debbie and I are down here," Ray tried to explain. "Like I said, Spike owes me a couple of grand—I was going to give it to Mo and hopefully buy some time. As for how I got on the hook in the first place, let's just say I'm an unlucky gambler."

"That's not all you're unlucky at," I said. "From what I've heard about Mo, he doesn't like to negotiate unless it's in *his* best interest, not the other way around. Good luck with that. In the meantime, we'll stay out at the Hideaway in La Quinta tonight and head back in the morning. I'm going to call my dad and fill him in and make arrangements for tomorrow. Have a drink, relax. We'll get some stuff and make dinner back at the Hideaway."

While Leo got up and snagged another round of beers out of Spike's cooler, I called Pop and filled him in. All he could say was "Wow. That's some progress. I'll see you tomorrow."

Yeah, tomorrow. *This is going to be fun*, I said to myself.

Leo gets payback.

CHAPTER 12

We stopped by the office on our way back to Manhattan Beach. Jacquie was sitting at her desk, looking as stunning as ever, wearing a light gray business suit and a fitted blouse in a beautiful blue color. It took me a few seconds to get words to come out of my mouth—she was just that pretty.

"Hi, gorgeous," I said. "You look very professional today. Is that a new outfit?"

"Yes," she said. "I decided I needed to spruce up my wardrobe a little bit. The clothes I wore as a dispatcher at the Sheriff's Department were okay since I never saw the public—or should I say, they never saw me! But here I'm the first person clients see, and I thought I should dress a little more professionally. Your dad agreed. And I even convinced him he should wear a tie when we are meeting clients."

"You do add a lot of class to this place," I said with a smile.

"I'll second that," Pop said, as he stuck his head through the open door and motioned everyone into his office. "You too, Jacquie."

As everyone moved to the inner office, I pulled Jacquie aside for a second.

"How about dinner tonight?" I asked her on the sly.

"Great," she said. "And I've been babysitting Fred, remember? Your cat? You can pick him up after dinner."

"Thank you—I owe you one."

"Yes, you do," she said with a wink as we joined the gang in Pop's office.

Leo, Ray, and Debbie were sitting in front of Pop's desk. Jacquie took the remaining club chair, and I sat on one of the credenzas in back.

Pop started things off. "All right, who wants to fill me in on why I spent a good portion of one of my rare days off running down license plates? Kit has filled me in on the basics, but now I want some solid details."

Since he was looking at me, and no one else volunteered, I spoke up first. "As you know, Ray and Debbie have been staying with Leo and his brother John at the beach. What none of us knew until Saturday night is that Ray here is on the lam from Vegas because he owes Mo Weinstein ten large."

"What about you, Debbie?" Pop asked, his eyes narrowing on the self-proclaimed singer.

Debbie stared down at her feet—I guessed she was feeling pretty silly right about now.

"Debbie was just along for the ride," I explained, figuring I'd save her some embarrassment. "Ray figured he could hide out down here until he could come up with the money. But unfortunately, Mo sent Vic Steckler and Frank Carpo, the two goons who roughed up Leo and John, to collect. Ray's been fortunate enough to be one step ahead of them. We're involved because Leo didn't know who else to turn to."

"It's a good thing I'm such a nice guy," Pop said with a chuckle.

I shrugged, then nodded with a smile.

"What were they doing down in Palm Springs?" Pop asked.

"Well, apparently, the guy that runs Sid's Lounge, a guy by the name of Spike, allegedly owes him some money and Ray here was going to use it to stall Mo for a while. I already told him that that probably wouldn't fly with Mo," I said.

"You've got that straight. Even if he took your money," Pop said looking at Ray, "he'd keep adding on vig and probably rough you up a little bit from time to time just as a warning. He'd have his hook into you for the rest of your life, that is if he let you live that long."

Pop looked back at me and said, "You did good getting Armstrong involved—he'll keep Mo's goons on ice for a while. That will give us some time to come up with a plan to deal with Mo. In the meantime, they'll be safe at Leo's for a day or two."

Then he turned to Ray again.

"You don't know how lucky you are. Leo and Kit are friends and Leo even works for me sometimes. That makes him family. So, for that reason and that reason alone we're going to try to get you out of this. Fortunately, I've dealt with Mo before and we might be able to come to some sort of understanding where you're concerned." Pop's face took on an extra stern look. "While I'm working on this, you and Debbie will do exactly as you're told. If you don't, I'll turn you loose, and you'll be on your own. Got that? On. Your. Own."

"Yes," they both answered sheepishly.

"Good," Pop said. Then, as he turned to me and Jacquie, his face softened. "The family's going down to the Hideaway this weekend. Would you and Jacquie like to come along? You too, Leo. As I said, you're family."

"Sure," Leo said. "And thanks."

"Yeah, thank you, Pop. You think I could bring three other people too?" I asked. "I'd like to invite Ron, Kathy, and Suzy from work to come along."

"Yeah," he said. "Why not. The more the merrier."

"You're the best," I told him. "I mean it."

Ignoring the flattery, he said, "Make sure to bring these two," as he pointed at Ray and Debbie with evident disdain. "That way we can keep an eye on them, and it'll give us more time to figure out a more long-term spot for them."

"Will do."

"Okay, meeting adjourned," he concluded. "See you all next weekend."

With that we all shook hands as we got up to leave. Leo, Ray, and Debbie went out to the hall and waited by the elevator while I said goodbye to Jacquie in a more appropriate manner. Though some might argue that it wasn't very work-setting appropriate, I was on cloud nine and could not have cared less.

I gave Leo a lift back to Manhattan Beach. Ray and Debbie followed in the Volkswagen. After everybody was safely back at Leo's place, I prepared to leave.

"I'll see all of you next weekend," I said to everyone, making sure it sounded like the direct order it was and not a matter of simple, *hope-to-see-you-there* well-wishing. And then I told Leo, "I'll call you later and we can discuss how we're going to get everyone down to La Quinta."

"Great! Can't wait. It should be fun. See you then," he said.

"Oh, and please, do whatever you can to make sure Ray and Debbie keep the hell out of trouble," I said.

"Like that'll do any good," he said, laughing. "I think you got a good idea by now what those two are like."

I just grimaced, rolled my eyes, and lamented, "Right. God help us! Well, catch you later." I was already fed up with the night club duo's screwy antics.

Then I headed back to town. It was about two in the afternoon when I arrived home. It was nice to be back. The place was a little stuffy, so I opened some windows and the sliding door to the balcony to let some air in. I grabbed another cold one out of the fridge, put some jazz on the stereo, plopped myself down on my favorite lounge chair, and tried to decide what I'd do with the last three days of my already busted vacation. Jacquie had to work so I couldn't take her away for a few days, but there was always dinner tonight. There was also the upcoming weekend, but I thought, alas, having all these people around was certainly going to cramp my style. Oh well, at least I was going to be with her. That seemed like all that mattered right now.

Since the day was pretty much over, I decided to just relax at home and then get ready for dinner with Jacquie. I wanted to take her someplace nice, so I made a reservation at a little French restaurant I knew. The owner, another old friend, promised me a nice cozy booth where we could dine in private, and I had no doubt it was going to be great.

Tomorrow, I was hoping, I could chill up at my sister Kay's house and lay out by her pool. Her husband, Joe, was a fireman and was gone a lot of the time due mostly to the scheduling of his time at the firehouse. And when Joe wasn't on duty at the firehouse, he was usually working his side job in construction. Kay would be working her day job too, so I'd have the whole place pretty much to myself unless one of her tennis friends had the same idea. On the one hand, I wouldn't mind if one or both of them did stop by. I speculated it would most likely be either Ladean or Gail, and they were both gorgeous and looked great in bikinis.

Yet the thought gave me some pause. Any other time, I would be more than happy to be in the company of a couple of hot babes— and technically available ones at that. But now, with Jacquie and me being an exclusive item, all I might have been interested in was to soak in the eye candy along with that great California sun, so I decided I wasn't going to care one way or the other. This was an unusual feeling for me. Suddenly, after all the chaos of the last few days, all I wanted to do was relax, listen to some good music, and have a cold drink or two, so I was kinda hoping they wouldn't show.

CHAPTER 13

I called the office to invite Kathy, Suzy, and Ron to La Quinta for the weekend.

"Yes, sounds terrific to me," Kathy said cheerfully, "and I just got off the phone with Jacquie and she invited us to join you two for dinner tonight."

"Oh, great," I said, doing my best to feign delight over this development. "We could all go out to dinner on the bank. You guys like steak? How about we meet at Damon's steak house in Glendale around eight?"

"Wonderful," she said. "We'll be there."

So much for my intimate dinner at the French restaurant. I had wanted Jacquie all to myself tonight, but there was always after dinner. I would take them to my favorite steak house instead. I called to cancel on the French place.

In those days, Damon's was in an old building on Central Avenue in Glendale. It was a long and narrow space that had a Polynesian motif. The steaks were always cooked just right, and they made a mean chi chi. The bar ran along one wall, and the booths were on a split level above along the opposite wall. I had my usual petite filet, blood rare, with rice. The house salad was great, and the garlic bread was fantastic—and they kept it coming. Everyone else had the same as me, except for Ron who decided he wanted prime rib.

We firmed up the plans for the weekend. Everyone was looking forward to lounging around the pool bagging rays. We could also drop in to the Cove and see Jacquie's dad while we were there.

"It'll be real nice to see Jacquie's dad again," Kathy said.

"Yeah, it's been way too long," Ron agreed.

'He'll be happy to see you two again too," Jacquie said. "He really likes both of you."

"We like him too," Kathy said, as Ron nodded in confirmation.

"We'll all have a good time," I said. "You can count on it."

"Never doubted it for a minute," Ron said, chuckling.

After dinner, Kathy and Ron took Suzy back to the apartment the bank had rented for her while she was in town. Jacquie and I were on our way to her place when she said, "You know, we've already had our third date, and you know what that means."

"Yeah," I said, "but I didn't know if you were ready to go there yet."

"I've arranged with your mom and dad for them to watch Nick and Fred tonight, so I'm all yours, but first we need to talk."

Here it goes, I thought to myself. *The Talk.*

"I've just been thinking . . . Where is it that you want this relationship to go?" she asked.

"Well, I'll tell you," I said. "We've known each other a long time, our dads being old war buddies and all. Our families get together all the time down at the desert."

"Yeah. They still do that," Jacquie said.

"I've palled around with your brothers plenty. When I left for active duty with the Navy, you were only fifteen, and back then I never would have expected to be here with you now."

"Well, you were quite the gentleman to not ogle a fifteen-year-old," Jacquie said, laughing.

"That I was. But when I saw you again a few months ago, after seven years, all I could think was, my, you're all grown up and how is it that I never noticed you before. That all changed during the time when you were helping on that case. When it was all over, I didn't want it to end."

"Neither did I," she said, "but then reality set in."

"It sure did. You had that great job with the Sheriff's Department, and I had my job at the bank. I couldn't ask you to quit yours, and I certainly wasn't going to quit mine. So, I reluctantly decided not to pursue it."

"I know," she said. "I felt the same way. Funny though, I never thought it was over. I somehow had this feeling things would work out."

"That's weird—I didn't either. Think it was over, I mean. I know both Mom and Pop knew how I felt about you and asked me what was going on. All I could say was, 'We'll see.' That's when I first, sort of casually, began suggesting to my dad that he should hire you away from the Sheriff's office and bring you to LA. Little did I know that he would actually do it.

"I thought about you a lot while I was cross training in London, and I made up my mind I was going to go down to Palm Springs and try to persuade you to come up to LA. I'm glad Pop stepped up—it would have been difficult with no job to offer you here, but then, there you were, in Pop's office. I thought to myself, 'Yes there is a God!'"

"You really thought that? That exact thing?"

"I did. And I know my mom was praying for it. Anyway, here we are, and since I can't tell the future, just know this—I couldn't be happier and I'm in it for the long haul."

"How do you know your mom was praying for it?" she asked.

"She told me so. She got her church group involved and all. It obviously works—she's been praying for my old man all her life, and it seems to have turned out okay for him. Besides, every time I see her, she says 'How's Jacquie?' in that tone with the wink, wink, nudge, nudge."

"She does?"

"She really likes you. We can't disappoint that nice old lady, now can we?"

"No," she said. "I guess we're going to your place."

With that I grabbed her and gave her a passionate kiss.

"Down boy," she said. "There will be time enough for that."

It's a good thing my apartment was close. We got there in record time.

When we got inside, Jacquie said, "Why don't you pour me a glass of wine and get yourself a drink, while I make myself a little more comfortable."

I grabbed one of my Czech Mickeys from the fridge, poured Jacquie a glass of Merlot, put some smooth jazz on the stereo, and went out onto the balcony. A few minutes later, Jacquie appeared wearing one of my chambray dress shirts, and not much else. She looked adorable.

"You don't mind?" she asked. "I just love these kinds of shirts and this one has your scent. Can I have it?"

"Sure," I said. "Good ol' Old Spice Classic. Gets 'em every time."

"Yeah," she said, "my dad wears it all the time."

"Yeah," I said, "best way to a woman's heart is to wear the same cologne her dad wears. Must be a Navy thing. My dad wears it, too."

We both had a chuckle and then cuddled on one of the lounge chairs. We never did get to the wine and beer. I don't kiss and tell, but let's just say I was a very happy camper that night.

CHAPTER 14

Pop called about 8:30 and woke me. I fumbled around for the phone and said, "Yeah?"

"Do you always answer the phone that way?" the voice on the other end said.

"Yeah, when whoever's calling wakes me up at 8:30 in the morning on my day off. Who's this?"

"It's me. Your father."

"Sorry, I'm half asleep," I teased him. "Didn't recognize your voice." I'd recognize his voice anywhere.

"Did you have a big night?" he asked.

I looked over at Jacquie lying next to me.

"You could say that." I was speaking softly so as not to wake her up. "By the way, Jacquie will be coming in a little late today."

"Oh, really?"

"Yeah, really," I said, "but you didn't call me this early to make small talk. What's up?"

"You're right," he said, clearing his throat. "I heard from Ricotta again yesterday. The meet is back on."

"When and where?" I asked.

"Under the pier in Manhattan Beach at seven tonight. He said come alone, of course, but I want you to take backup with you anyway. You know the drill."

"Okay. I'll come by the office later and pick up the envelope."

"Copy that," he said. "Oh, and about that other thing—tell her to come in whenever she's ready, and congratulations."

"Thanks, Pop," I said.

"Your mother will be very happy," he said as he hung up.

Jacquie had slept through the call—not even a muscle stirred or an eye batted. She definitely needed more sleep. I gave her a gentle kiss on the forehead, trying not to wake her. I succeeded, then drifted off after watching her peaceful face for a few minutes.

My mother may be very happy indeed, but not as happy as I was. Not even close.

We both rolled out of bed around ten. She showered first, then me. While she was in the shower, I called Leo and asked him if he could act as backup that night. He said sure.

"Meet me at the pizza joint up on the corner of your street at 5:30," I said.

"You got it. See you then," he said. "And why don't you invite Marco along—we could use another hand, and I don't think he's working tonight."

"Great idea," I said. "It's been a couple of weeks since we were down at your place. It'd be great to have him along. And yeah, he does like his pizza and beer."

"He sure does. Catch you later," he said with a laugh and hung up.

Jacquie was still in the shower, so I had time for another call to Marco.

"*Hola*," Marco's mom said cheerfully when she answered the phone.

"Hola, Senora Rams, esta Marco alla?" I asked.

"Si, una momento, por favor," she said then hollered to another room, *"Marquito, esta su amigo Kit en el telefono."*

"Gracias, Mama," he said as he picked up the phone. "What's up, dude?" he asked.

"Oh, not much," I said. "Leo tells me you're off tonight. Is that true and if so, would you like to pick up a little extra money and act as our backup tonight? There's pizza and beer in it for you too," I laughed.

"Damn," he said. "The bank just called me about ten minutes ago and told me I had to come in tonight. I can't tell them no, as much as I'd like to. What's the caper?"

"Too bad you can't make it, but you're going to love this," I said. "Has Leo mentioned anything about Ray and Debbie and our little adventure out in Palm Springs last weekend?"

"No, all I know is that he called in sick on Monday, something about a little accident and black eye and split lip," he said.

"Now I know you're going to love this," I said.

"Go on, I can't wait," he said.

"Well, Leo and I found out the hard way that their only reason for being down here in California is that they're hiding from a Vegas loan shark. Except that loan shark sent a couple of goons after them. To make a long story short, Ray and Debbie took off for Palm Springs, and when the two goons showed up at Leo's place and they weren't there they gave Leo a black eye and a split lip, kidnapped John, and tossed Leo's pad."

"WOW, no way!" he said with astonishment.

"Yes way," I said. "But that's not the half of it. We tracked Ray and Debbie down to a bar in the Springs, where they were supposed to meet up with a guy named Spike who runs a bar down there, but the two goons apparently got there first and roughed up

Spike too. We were fortunate enough to get them put on ice before Ray and Debbie arrived."

"Sounds exciting, but if you got them off the board, what do you need me for?" he asked.

"Another little case that I'm working for Pop," I said. "One of our clients is being blackmailed, and I'm making the money exchange tonight under the Manhattan Beach Pier. I thought you might like some serious free pizza and beer, then join Leo as my backup."

"I really can't. Even if you'd have called before the bank, I would've had to back out on you guys," he said. "But I want to hear more about this Ray and Debbie thing."

"Oh, you will, and don't worry about tonight—Leo and I have got it. Although it would have been nice to have you along."

"Thanks, it would've been nice to be there. Catch you later," he said.

"Later," I said as I hung up.

"Who were you talking to?" Jacquie asked as she came out of the shower, wearing nothing but a smile.

"Oh," I said, trying to wipe the Cheshire cat grin off my face. "I just got through lining up Leo for tonight. I tried to get Marco to join us too, but he has to work."

"You'll have to introduce us sometime," she said.

"You can count on it," I said. "Maybe after all of this crap is over, we can get the gang together. Maybe for another day at the beach."

"Hmmm, sounds like fun," she said. "The shower is all yours."

"Thanks," I said, giving her a little peck on the cheek as I headed into the bathroom. "Would you like to join me?" I asked wearing a big grin.

She just smiled and said, "No, I don't think so. If I start taking another shower, I'll never get to work."

"Pop did say to take all the time you needed," I said, as my grin got even wider.

"Well, I'm glad he's so understanding, but I don't think so. Now *go*," she said as she snapped at me with her towel.

"Okay," I said, trying not to sound too disappointed as I headed for the bathroom.

After I showered and dressed, I took Jacquie home to her place so she could change clothes.

As she was getting out of the car, I said, "I'll see you at the office around four or so. I have to pick up the envelope again."

She gave me a quick kiss and said, "See you there."

I couldn't wait till it was four o'clock!

———

After I kissed Jacquie again for good luck and picked up the envelope, I headed for Manhattan Beach. I arrived at the pizza joint around five. Since I was early, I ordered a large half-and-half pizza. I knew Leo liked pepperoni on his, so I made it half pepperoni and half sausage, mushrooms, and sautéed onions for me. I ordered a couple of beers too. Leo showed up right on time—the waitress delivered the steaming pizza just as Leo sat down. The aroma was mind-bending.

"How did you know?" he asked.

"Lucky guess. Besides, no reason we should have to work on an empty stomach," I said.

"True. Very true."

As we ate, we got down to business.

"Here's the plan," I said. "We'll take my car over and park in the pier's lot. We're supposed to meet Ricotta under the pier. We'll both go in. You're my backup so you'll try to stay outta sight, but somewhere where you can watch my back."

"Okay," he said. "Got it."

"Since I've already been shot at once trying to deal with this guy, we're going in armed. Just like out at the Springs. You'll take my 9mm. You do remember how to use that?" I teased.

"Yeah, I remember," he said with a grin.

With that, we lifted our glasses in a toast. "To a successful evening," I said.

"To a successful evening," he responded, and we downed our drinks.

When we arrived at the drop, I managed to find a parking spot close to the place where you could go down under the pier. I popped my trunk and grabbed my .38 and strapped it to my belt, then handed the 9mm to Leo. I grabbed a couple pairs of cuffs, just in case, and a couple of flashlights. When I felt like I had everything and was all set to head in, I turned to Leo.

"Give me a five-minute head start and then follow me in. Try not to be seen; stay in the shadows as much as you can."

"Got it," he said.

I was about thirty feet in when a muffled voice said, "You got the package?"

"Yeah," I said. "You got yours?"

"Yeah."

"Step out here where I can see you."

I flashed my light toward the voice. I couldn't believe my eyes. There, .38 special in hand, was none other than my old pal Ray Ricco!

"*WHAT THE FUCK!?* Is Ricco short for Ricotta?" I asked. "Is Debbie involved in this too?"

"Yes," another voice said, as Debbie herself came out into the open, also sporting a .38 special. I think they were even more surprised than I was.

"I told you to stay hidden," Ray hissed at Debbie.

"Why? I think he knows who we are now."

Then I looked at Ray. He was obviously scared to death now, making him much more dangerous. I really had to proceed with caution.

"What were you planning on doing with that .38 in your hand?" I asked. "Didn't anybody tell you not to point a gun at someone unless you intend to use it, which I don't think you do, Ray. You'd both better give me the guns before you hurt yourselves . . . or me—and I wouldn't like that at all. You got some serious explaining to do."

"Uh, I don't think so," Ray said as he raised his gun nervously, hand shaking, as if he were going to shoot.

"No!" Debbie yelled, still holding her gun, though not pointing it at anyone in particular.

"You'd better listen to her," Leo said as he stepped from the shadows.

Ray started to waver, shifting the gun from one target to the other. By this time, I had my .38 out and aimed at him.

"Don't even think about it. You won't make it out of here alive if you do. Both of you give me your guns now," I said.

He had the look of a deer caught in the headlights. He slowly began to raise his left hand in the air while reaching out with his right to hand me the gun.

"Butt first," I said. "Don't want that thing going off accidentally and hurting someone. 'Specially me."

Debbie handed over her gun without an ounce of hesitation. She seemed eager to get rid of it, like it was on fire or something.

After Leo and I collected their weapons, I cuffed both of them and said, "As much as I'd like to hear your explanation, I don't really want to hear it twice, so we'll save it for tomorrow. You can explain it to Pop, our lawyer, and our client. In the meantime, we're going to stash you someplace where you can't disappear again."

I took them to my car. Just to be ornery, I told our two enter-tainers-turned-gangsters that there really wasn't enough room for two in the back seat of a Mustang, and I stuffed Ray in the trunk, putting Debbie in the backseat. Truth was, they both could have fit in the backseat even if it would have been tight. But con-sidering all the trouble these two had caused Leo and me since Saturday night, basically I wanted to scare the shit out of them as punishment. In fact, I'd have thrown them both in the trunk if I thought they'd fit without suffocating. I guess my tactic worked because Debbie cried all the way back to Leo's place. We took them inside, tossed them onto a couch still handcuffed, and then Leo and I grabbed a couple of beers while I called Pop and filled him in.

"No shit," was his response. "This caper gets stranger and stranger by the minute."

"You can say that again," I said. "Hopefully, we can sort it out when we meet tomorrow."

"I'll have Jack and Fat Al in my office . . . let's say around ten?" he asked.

"Ten is good enough for me. In the meantime, where can I stash these two sorry-ass blackmailers so that they can't run away again?"

"Take them to the safehouse on San Fernando Road. The one underneath the 10 freeway. Big Eddie and his sons will take care of them until you can pick them up in the morning and bring them here."

"Copy that," I said and hung up.

The safehouse was in a trailer park run by one of Pop's opera-tives by the name of Big Eddie Garcia. He'd come by the nickname honestly. Both he and his twin sons were big enough to pass for the entire defensive line of the USC football team and they wouldn't have needed anybody else.

I stuffed Ray back in the trunk, and Debbie promised to behave herself on the ride into town, so I left Leo at his home to go about the rest of his evening. I dropped Ray and Debbie off with Big Eddie. Ray looked half pissed and half scared out of his pants, Debbie looked like she was about to cry again, and together the pathetic pair looked like they hadn't been sleeping very well and smelled like they needed a shower. It was doubtful they would get much of either here, but that wasn't my problem now.

"Feel free to hurt them if they get out of line," I said as I handed them over, smiling at Ray and Debbie while making sure they heard that.

"You got it, bro," Big Eddie said as he grinned at them like an overeager hit man in a mob movie.

You could tell they didn't know whether or not I was kidding. That's exactly the way I wanted to leave them. And I'm not entirely sure I was.

I couldn't wait until tomorrow to start sorting this whole thing out. I was really curious about their connection to our dead guy, Lester Sloan, and how much of this had anything to do with Ray Ricco's debt to Mo Weinstein. I probably wouldn't get much sleep tonight thinking about it. Unless I had a few more beers to make me sleepy. What a great idea—and I got on it as soon as I got home.

CHAPTER 15

Before I left the trailer park, I arranged for Big Eddie to drop Ray and Debbie off at Pop's office. I was tired of being the guy doing all the running around on this ridiculous caper. So I headed straight to Pop's office the next morning, arriving at around ten. Jacquie was at her desk, and I gave her a quick kiss before I went into Pop's office. Ray and Debbie were seated in a couple of clearly uncomfortable folding chairs, looking like a couple of captured soldiers from a war zone awaiting their interrogation. Pop was behind his desk smoking one of his Cuban cigars. It was amazing the volume of smoke he could produce from one of those things, like he was a human steel mill. Uncle Jack, Fat Albert, and Max were sitting off to the side in the more hospitable club chairs—they too were smoking Cohibas. The room looked like Pittsburgh.

"Where's mine?" I asked.

Pop just pointed silently to the humidor and motioned for me to take a seat.

Just as I sat down in the remaining club chair, without any

prompting from anyone, Debbie started to explain. It was a bomb-shell of an explanation.

"I'm your daughter," she blurted out, looking at Uncle Jack.

The room fell silent. So silent that for a fleeting second, I thought everyone had actually, physically stopped breathing, as if suddenly there was no oxygen in the room to breathe.

Holy crap! I thought to myself. *She's my freakin' cousin!* I was so glad I didn't take her up on her offer that night at the beach.

Uncle Jack bore an expression on his face like none I'd ever seen on a human being before or since. A mixture of shock and disbelief; he never had a clue that Ruth might be pregnant. Would he have done anything differently if he had known? He couldn't honestly say, but the sudden mind-altering revelation of the truth was a gut punch. Guilt, regrets, and old memories all came flooding back in one fell swoop. He just sat there in silence taking it all in.

"You're Ruth Roman's daughter?" he finally asked in a monotone.

"Ruth Roman Long," Debbie sobbed. "She got married shortly after she went to New York. But she was two months pregnant with me when she left Las Vegas after the faked car accident, and after the false reports hit the papers that she had died in the collision.

"The way mom explained it to me, she said she never told you because the two of you were breaking up. But I think she never told you because she was afraid; afraid of the dangerous people you associated with back in those days. Afraid for the safety of her baby. She was afraid that if you knew, you'd come after her and me, if you even let her go in the first place.

"Only now, here I am," Debbie concluded.

"Well, this is something of a shock," Pop said, trying to lighten the tension. "Please go on."

"When Mom was dying of cancer, she told me the whole story," Debbie said, nervously fidgeting in her chair. "She even gave me some journals, newspaper clippings, and a sea chart that she said had something to do with a gold robbery back in the old days."

"Your turn," Pop said sternly, his eyes narrowing on Uncle Jack and Fat Albert. "You want to fill me in?"

Uncle Jack shifted uncomfortably in his chair. "Back in '39, there was a robbery on the *Rex*," he said. "About one million dollars in gold at 1939 prices in transit—a shipment from Sicily to the Dragna mob in LA was on board the *Rex*. Money that was supposed to be protected from Mussolini. It was a pretty slick job, I have to admit. A bunch of guys boarded the *Rex* from a speedboat, snatched the gold from the counting room safe, and took off across the ocean just like a bunch of pirates from a Douglas Fairbanks movie."

"I remember hearing about that when I was still a cop," Pop said. "Nobody put much stock in it."

"It's true," Uncle Jack said. "The mob always held Tony and me responsible, even though we didn't take it. It was rumored that this was what Tony and Nick Colleti were arguing about the night Tony died. The mob was trying to take over our Vegas hotel and casino—Tony and me were partners in that venture—as payment for the gold."

"Did the mob threaten you?" I asked Uncle Jack.

"No, not directly, because I was Tony's silent partner. He was the front man and got all the pressure. At the same time, he always suspected Nick was the inside man on the robbery and threatened to give him up to the mob. Nick retaliated by threatening to kill Tony. Ruthie witnessed the whole thing. When Tony died so abruptly, there was wild speculation that it wasn't a heart attack, but that he was actually poisoned by a rival. A lot of that sensational speculation made the papers."

At this point, Uncle Jack paused and laughed weakly. "Believe me, if any of those folks could have seen the way Tony drank and the crap that he ate, nobody would question the plain fact that his heart exploded.

"Anyway, Ruthie bought into the rumors and was convinced that Nick was responsible, somehow and some way, for killing Tony. She also convinced herself that Nick was going to kill her because she knew too much, and he wanted to silence her for good. Crazy stuff, but she came to me and begged me to help her disappear. What could I do? I arranged the phony accident and sent her off to New York. This Lester Sloan, the guy who was shot right in front of Kit the other night, he was the reporter that covered both incidents."

Pop turned back to Debbie. "Other than being the reporter that covered Tony's death and, umm, what he must have thought was your mother's passing I guess, what's his connection to you? And why was he the contact at the first drop instead of Ray?"

"As I said before, when my mom died, I found all the journals and the news clippings; most of the articles had Lester's byline. It was ironic, really. For a long time, I had wanted to go to Las Vegas and try to get a job as a singer. Plans my mother disapproved of, for obvious reasons. But now that she was gone, well . . . there was nothing holding me back. So I took the package of articles with me, I guess because I didn't have much else to bring with me, really. When I arrived in Vegas, I got myself a job at Nick Colleti's casino as a lounge singer, working with Ray here. I guess I must look a lot like my mother because Lester—who was hanging out at Nick's—recognized the resemblance and approached me."

"You do look like your mother," Jack said forlornly. "She was a beautiful woman. Too bad she had to go through so much. 'Specially cancer. Did she suffer much?"

"No, she went very fast," Debbie said, looking away as if signaling that she wanted to avoid the subject, her gaze now landing on Pop. "Anyway, Lester kept harping on me," she continued. "At first, I insisted I wasn't Ruth Roman's daughter. Until I finally broke down and admitted it. It was later on, when Lester found out I had kept all of the journals and his old news clippings, that he came up with the idea to help Ray out by blackmailing him." She pointed at Uncle Jack. "Ray and I were getting close to each other, if you know what I mean."

"Yeah, we kinda figured that out," I said with a smile and a laugh. It brought a few chuckles from the group.

She just glared at me and continued with her tale.

"*And*, with him owing that Mo fella money, Ray and me thought that would be a good way to pay his debt, so we went along with Lester's plan. Besides, we figured that going to LA would be a good place to hide from Mo's collectors while we got the money. But then Lester came up with the idea to go searching for the gold instead, saying that we should just use the blackmail money to finance it. You see, he'd seen that chart I told you about. He claimed it showed exactly where the gold is, under the ocean off, what is it, Catalina Island, I think. Lester said that once we got the gold, we could easily pay off Ray's debt and have millions to split three ways among ourselves."

"All of that seems to add up," I said. "But you still haven't explained why he was our first contact and not Ray. That's what I'd really like to know."

"Ray and I went to Manhattan Beach to find this Captain Pete who had made up the original charts—that's where we met John, and that's how we wound up staying with John's brother Leo at his place. You know, where we first met you?

"We were to meet up with Lester back on Mt. Washington for the money drop. But just as we were arriving at the location, we saw two guys leaving in a blue Dodge. We didn't know who they were or why they were there, but Ray suspected that they might be Mo Weinstein's leg breakers, he called them, looking for us. What can I say? We got scared and went back down to your friend Leo's place to hide."

"It's starting to make a little sense," I said. "Ray's suspicion was spot on. Steckler and Carpo were looking for them and had probably roughed up Lester in the process. He would have told them about Captain Pete, who in turn would have told them about John."

Pop pondered what he'd been hearing for a long moment. Then he asked pointedly, "Ms. Long, do you know that Lester Sloan is dead?"

"What?" she said, a look of authentic shock on her face. "Who did it?"

"Oh my God!" Ray exclaimed.

"We don't know yet," Pop said, "but if it wasn't you two, Steckler and Carpo are the most likely suspects. Or at least they were, up until a few moments ago."

Then Pop looked at me and said, "I think you're right, Kit. I think those goons roughed up Lester Sloan, looking for the money, perhaps. That's why the place was a mess when you got there. But I don't think they killed him. They would have had no reason to kill him. Thing is, I can't imagine why anyone would have a reason to kill him."

Debbie Long was obviously getting a bit scared now—you could see her shaking and about ready to cry. If those two goons had killed Lester, they'd likely have no hesitation in killing both her and Ray if he didn't pay up. It was good for her to be aware of this reality—the girl was playing with fire.

I handed her some Kleenex and tried to calm her down. "It's all right," I assured her. "You're safe as long as you're with us."

Pop mused out loud. "Hmmm. Speaking of Ray's debt, don't Mo Weinstein and his cronies provide muscle for Nick Colleti, among their other, uh, enterprises?" he asked, looking at Uncle Jack and Fat Albert. Both men nodded.

Pop then turned to Ray and questioned, "And you really owe Nick the ten Gs?"

"Yeah," Ray said.

"So," Pop continued the thread, "when we were to deliver the ten grand to an 'R. Ricotta,' I'm assuming that's you."

"Yeah," Ray said again.

"What a cheesy alias you picked," I said. No one laughed. "Tough crowd," I said.

"This is serious," Pop scolded.

Pop just shook his head and continued. "So there never was any 'package' for our man, which is to say Kit, to pick up. You were just going to rob him of the ten grand and think that would be the end of it, am I right?"

Ray and Debbie nodded in dumb silence, as if finally recognizing the stupidity of their so-called plan.

"All we really had was the manila envelope of newspaper articles that I brought from New York and gave to Lester," Debbie offered apologetically, as if she felt compelled to answer Pop's question. "And now I don't even know where that is," she added.

"Boy, oh boy," Pop groaned. "You two are a piece of work! So we found Lester Sloan instead of you two, and now Lester Sloan is dead. And by the way, we have your envelope. We found it in Sloan's apartment after he was murdered."

I said to Pop, "Do you think Steckler and Carpo killed Sloan and it was those guys I heard leaving the scene?"

"Could be," he said, stroking his chin thoughtfully.

"So where was the blue car when you saw it?" I asked Ray.

"Just like Debbie said, these two guys, I'm guessing this Steckler and Carpo you're talking about, they were just leaving in that beat-up blue Dodge."

"Good guess." I said to Pop, "They were probably just moving it when Ray and Debbie saw them. Because I didn't see it anywhere around there, not parked out front, and the side streets were empty at that hour."

"So," I continued, now looking at Ray and Debbie, "Ray, what made you suspicious of the two guys leaving Mt. Washington, if you didn't know who they were?

"Look," he said, "I owe Mo Weinstein ten large. You don't need to be a genius to know he would be sending someone after me to collect. I just figured Steckler and Carpo were them, even if I didn't know for sure."

"Well, we both know you're no genius," I said mockingly. "You didn't know we'd caught up with Mo's goons and put them on ice for a while, yet you called to schedule another meet; so why did you feel it was safe to try the blackmail again?"

"Well," Ray said nervously. "We really didn't have much choice at that point, don't you see? We were desperate, I still owed Mo, and time was running out. I guess we figured that we'd managed to avoid them up until then, and we hoped we could stay ahead of them for a little while longer. You know, until we could get the seed money from your uncle to finance the operation to retrieve the gold. Once we did that, we could pay off Mo—with interest even, if he insisted—we'd all be rich, and everybody would be happy.

"But when we blew the first drop, and, well, we didn't hear anything from Lester—I mean, we didn't know he was killed of course—that's shocking news to us—I guess we kind of pan-icked. We took off for Palm Springs to try to get some money from Spike, the guy who runs Sid's Lounge down there, money that he owes me. We hoped to use that money to buy some extra time from Mo. But when we failed to get any money from Spike, we figured we'd arrange another drop to get the ten grand; we were going to do it ourselves and figured we'd meet up with Lester again afterward." Ray appeared painfully aware of the irony of those last words. "Guess that's not going to happen," he concluded.

Pop had sat silent through Ray's whole sad speech. I could see that he was pondering things only a savvy detective would think about. Finally, he spoke up.

"So the two of you met with Captain Pete in Manhattan Beach, is that correct?"

Ray and Debbie nodded.

"And what exactly did you talk to him about?"

"Nothing," Debbie exclaimed, obviously starting to feel a little guilty. "We just showed him the chart and told him where we wanted to go. In a boat, I mean. That's all—*really.*"

"Oh, shit!" Uncle Jack bellowed, jumping to his feet and slamming his hand on Pop's desk. "You morons!" he yelled, and then he glared directly at Debbie Long as he mimicked her voice in sing-song sarcasm, "'*Oh, we told him nothing, we just showed him this cute little chart and told him we want to go sailing.*' Holy fuck!"

Jack was beginning to lose his cool.

"Easy Jack," Pop said, trying to calm him.

But Jack would have none of it. Still glaring like a demon at Ray and Debbie, he continued to rant. "Don't you realize that by telling him '*nothing*' you've basically told him everything? You do realize he was sailing master on the *Rex* when that robbery happened, don't you? And that he was the one who piloted the boat that the Colleti brothers used to chase down the robbers!? Or didn't you know that little fact? He drew up the goddamn chart, for chrissake!"

"Easy Jack," Pop repeated, and for a long moment the room was silent as Jack slowly sank back into his seat, like a balloon slowly deflating.

"Well," I said, shaking my head and hoping once again to break the tension. "I guess we'll have to pay ol' Captain Pete a visit. Seems like the only sensible next step."

"Sounds that way," Pop said, shrugging his shoulders.

"I'm going to take a ride down to Manhattan Beach," I said. "Anybody want to join me?"

"Yes," everybody said in unison, as they rose from their chairs, eager to get going.

I looked at Ray and asked, "I just have one more question. At any time before last night, did you have any idea who I was?"

"No," he said. "We had no idea you were related to Jack. We were just as surprised as you were when we saw you under the pier. We just thought you were a friend of Leo's."

"This can't be real—there aren't supposed to be coincidences," I said. "At least not ones this big."

"Well, that's what it is," he said, looking as confused as I felt. "Just a coincidence."

"We'll have to deal with who killed Lester later. Dealing with Captain Pete is more important right now," Pop said, rising from his desk and shaking his head. "I'm too old for this shit."

As Pop and the others left the office, Uncle Jack remained seated for a moment, staring into space like a man in a trance. I knew immediately what he was thinking about, and I tried to offer some comfort.

"So if her daughter is any indication," I said gently, "I gather this Ruth Roman was pretty damn gorgeous and a wonderful woman."

"She was," Uncle Jack intoned.

"So tell me Unc, when did you realize that Debbie Long was Ruth's daughter?"

And without looking at me, still staring straight ahead into the unforgiving cosmos, Uncle Jack said, "I knew it the instant I set eyes on her."

CHAPTER 16

Leo arrived in the parking lot just as we were leaving. I rolled down the window and gave him the scoop.

"Just turn yourself around and follow behind," I said. "We're headed to Captain Pete's."

Pop, Uncle Jack, Max, Ray, and Debbie followed in Pop's big-ass Olds Delta 88. Traffic sucked on a Thursday afternoon. Who am I kidding? It always sucked. So it took us about an hour and a half to make the trip from Pasadena to Manhattan Beach. Leo and I arrived first. We found Captain Pete behind the bar and waved as we entered.

Pete waved back. "Hey there," he greeted us. "You guys goin' divin' this weekend or did you just come in to have a cold one?"

"Maybe both," I said.

Then the door opened behind me and in came Pop, Uncle Jack, and Max, with Debbie and Ray in tow. The look of surprise on Captain Pete's face was a dead giveaway.

Pop said, "Hi, Pete. I think you know these two. We need to have a little chat."

Captain Pete turned a nice shade of pink, faster than a chameleon, and pointed to a booth big enough for all of us to sit.

Pop started the conversation. "I understand these two have been trying to solicit your aid in a little diving expedition and they showed you a map with the destination they want to go to. Does that chart by any chance look a little familiar to you?" He gave the captain a quizzical look that made it clear he was serious about getting a straight answer. Hell, Pop's look told Pete he *already knew* the answer.

All Captain Pete could say was "Uh, yeah, I guess it does."

"So, what was the plan?" Pop said. "What were you planning to do, Pete? Help them find the gold and kill them, or just figure out a way to cheat them out of it?"

"Hold on, Frenchy!" Pete protested. "I never killed nobody—you know that. I was just going to take them on a wild goose chase like I did Tony when we went looking for it back in the old days. When they got tired of looking then I was going to go back and get it," he said.

"You were going to go back and get it just like you were going to do to Tony back in the day? What I wanna know is, why didn't you do it *back in the day?*" Pop demanded, scowling.

"Well . . . I . . ." Pete stuttered.

"Go on, spit it out," Pop seethed.

Captain Pete started in again. "Well. Look, you might as well know it now . . . Nick, his brother Tommy, and I were in on the heist together. Nick and Tommy weren't sailors. They didn't know shit about navigation or anything. So, they hired six ex-Navy buddies of mine to do the heist, and Nick, Tommy, and I were the ones who went after them in the launch. We went to our rendezvous point. We buried the gold on San Nicholas Island, and then we motored north of Catalina where we dynamited the speedboat.

When we got back to the *Rex*, we told Jack here and later Tony, when he returned from his business trip in Vegas, that the gold was lost off Catalina. Naturally, I faked the charts."

Uncle Jack was fuming as he listened to this, but for now he held his cool.

"Were the crew members that went with you on the chase in on it?" Pop asked.

Captain Pete leaned back in the booth with a broad, satisfied grin on his face.

"Well, you see, that was the real genius of the plan," he said. "In all the confusion of that night, neither Jack nor anybody else on the *Rex* noticed that only three of the so-called pirates got on the pirate speedboat with the gold—and the night's cash receipts, as well, I might add. The three sailors that Nick, Tommy, and me took on the launch, those were the other three ex-Navy guys that Nick had already embedded in the ship's crew. So of course, those were the guys he grabbed to join us on the 'chase,'" Pete motioned air quotes with his hands when he said the word *chase*.

"Unbelievable," Pop uttered.

"Then what happened?" I asked.

"Tony tried finding it, but of course he couldn't because it wasn't where he thought. So eventually he just gave up. Besides, by this time the County was trying to close him down and was regularly raiding his ship, so he had his hands full just trying to evade the law. And while Nick held on to the charts for 'safekeeping,' before he, Tommy, and I could go back for it, the Japs bombed Pearl Harbor, the Navy closed off all diving in the channel, and access to San Nicholas was prohibited. Still is," he said. "Why Nick kept the logs and charts, I don't know, unless it was in case the Dragna mob came after him. Anyway, we didn't need them to find the gold. We just had to get back onto San Nicholas and we can't."

"So," Pop said, "when Ms. Long and her pal Ray here showed up with the logs and charts, you thought you could take their money, go back, sneak on to the island, and get the gold. Just how were you planning on doing that?"

"I hadn't quite figured out that far," Pete said, scratching his beard.

Uncle Jack, who had been listening intently to the captain's tale, as the blood in his veins quietly boiled all the while, finally spoke.

"Sneaking on to that island wouldn't be too smart. The Navy would catch you in a heartbeat. But there might be another way. I still have some connections in Washington. One of them is on the Armed Services Committee. Maybe I can get a diving permit for, oh, say, a salvage operation—or even better—for an archaeological expedition to San Nicholas Island and its surrounds."

That got a good laugh and a thumbs up from all.

Pop said, "Okay, Captain Pete, my brother will get us a permit, and for the time being, you're in, but you better not try to cross us. If you do, I might turn you over to Nick Colleti and let him deal with you."

"I won't," he said. "But, just out of curiosity, how *are* you going to deal with Nick Colleti?"

"I don't quite know yet," Pop said, "but having that gold will give us a better bargaining position."

"*Amen!*" I said. "It sure will."

"Okay," Pop said to Uncle Jack, "the ball's in your court. Talk to your connection and get us a permit, and then we'll go treasure hunting."

"It may take a couple of weeks," Uncle Jack said. "Stuff like this doesn't get the green light overnight. I'll do my best to get things rolling."

"Okay," Pop said as he turned to Captain Pete. "You, my

friend, will supply all the necessary equipment. You know where it's buried, so I expect you know exactly what we'll need to unbury it. We'll tell you when to deliver it to my boat. You know where it's kept down in Fleitz Brothers Marina?"

"Yep," the captain said. "I'm familiar with the spot. I'll have everything we need ready when you want it. Just let me know."

With that we had a round or two of beers on the captain and I started thinking about the coming weekend down at the Hideaway. We were going to have quite a crowd.

CHAPTER 17

I had the Bronco loaded again. Ron met Kathy, Suzy, and me at the bank and from there we drove to Jacquie's place to pick her up. Then we made the trek to La Quinta.

After settling in we headed over to the Cove to see Jacquie's dad and get some refreshments.

When we arrived, Jacquie's dad was in his usual position behind the bar.

"Hi, Jack," I said as we entered.

"Hi, yourself," he said as he came around to greet us.

Jacquie gave her dad a hug and a kiss and briefly introduced everyone. While the others settled down in a couple of booths, I stayed at the bar to get us some drinks. When we were alone, he asked, "Who's this Suzy? She looks so much like Jacquie."

Shockingly, I hadn't realized it till this moment, but the resemblance was uncanny. I gave him the rundown on how I met her briefly in London, and that she was here for cross training at the bank. I also told him what we had learned on the sailing trip about Suzy's mom having worked during the war as a Royal Naval attaché to U.S. Navy Intelligence. You should have seen the look on his face when I told him.

"What's wrong, Jack?" I asked. "You look like you've just seen a ghost."

Apparently, Pop wasn't the only friend Jack made while in London, and he and Pop did indeed know Suzy's mom, Melanie. The world kept getting smaller and smaller. With her husband off in Burma, also with the Royal Navy, Melanie and Jack had quickly become "very good friends," to use Jack's words. She became pregnant with Suzy. Since she was a married woman, she let everyone believe the baby was her husband's. She even convinced Jack that the baby was her husband's and not his.

At any rate, they broke the relationship off, and she resigned from the Royal Navy to have her child. When the war in Europe ended, both Pop and Jack returned to the States, where Jack started his own family. Suzy never knew the truth. Evidently, Melanie did send a letter to Jack years later, finally admitting to him that he was Suzy's father, but by then, he had his own family here, and Suzy was comfortable in thinking Melanie's Royal Navy husband was her father. Why rock the boat? Now here was Suzy in the flesh.

"What should I do?" he asked.

"That's a tough one," I said. "I'm not very good at giving personal advice."

I knew that Jack was now divorced from Ruby, Jacquie's mom, so I imagined that letting the secret out couldn't do any harm there, and I told him so.

Jack nodded, adding, "Thing is, I didn't even know Ruby when I had the affair with Melanie."

"Maybe you should tell both Suzy and Jacquie together," I said. "You still have that letter Suzy's mom wrote you, right?"

"Yes," he said.

"Then take them both privately aside sometime this weekend and let them read it," I suggested. "Jacquie should know she has a sister, and so should Suzy. It's only fair to the both of them."

"You're right," he said. "I'll dig it out when I get home and show it to them tomorrow."

"Sounds like a plan," I said, and went back to the group to have some nachos and beer. Things started to make sense. As Pop always told me, there is no such thing as a coincidence.

CHAPTER 18

When we arrived back at the Hideaway, the evening was still young. We decided to light a blaze in the firepit and sit outside around the pool.

The house was originally built in the late teens or early '20s by my Grandpa Harry and had some definite personality. Grandpa had moved to the area after retiring as Sheriff of Beatty, Nevada. He got the land cheap and built a little horse ranch that he named Harry's Hideaway. Over the years, it just became the Hideaway. The house was built in the Santa Fe style with some art deco features. When Grandpa died in 1950, Pop took over and started to renovate and bring the house up to mid-century standards.

Then, in 1958, when they started buying land for the new La Quinta Country Club, Pop made a killing selling off the bulk of the ranch property to the developers. Pop used a good portion of his profits to turn the house into a small, private family resort. One of the nicest lots, the one right next door to the Hideaway, he sold to Jacquie's dad, who, for whatever reason, perhaps sheer gratitude, built a smaller version of the Hideaway, also in the Santa Fe style.

Since she grew up there, she loved the style of her own house, but Jacquie simply adored the Hideaway, with its warm adobe color and for contrast, window frames and doors painted turquoise blue. It was a great place to get away from telephones and office buildings and LA traffic and spend a few days kicking back.

"I always loved that blue trim around the windows," Jacquie said. "My dad should do the same to his house."

"You don't want him to be too much of a copycat," I said, poking her gently. "After all, your dad's place is laid out pretty much exactly like ours."

"I know," she said. "But this place is so much more of a party house."

"You do know this is a family house, and by family, I mean all my uncles, aunts, and cousins can use this place anytime they want. Pop may be the primary beneficiary of the place and made all the upgrades, but Grandpa Harry left it to the whole family to enjoy, not just us."

"Well, maybe I'll be part of the family someday," she said with that not-so-subtle "hint, hint" look in her eye.

I just looked at her, smiled, and said, "You just never know. We'll have to discuss that later."

"That's promising," she said, smiling back.

The Hideaway was laid out in the shape of an H. The main entrance was inset in the little portico created by the feet of the H. Upon entering the front door, the expansive country kitchen extended to the left, the home office and guest bathroom were on the right. The bar of the H constituted the main rooms of the house, principally the dining room, living room, and pantry. The rest of the H was a meticulously designed sprawl of bedrooms, several of them with private full baths, extending down either side of an interior courtyard, and a glistening swimming pool.

All of the bedrooms were connected by wide and spacious interior hallways, but you could also access any one of them from the courtyard pool area.

Naturally, the interior was given the same Santa Fe treatment—the same adobe finish on the walls, and the floors were all distressed wood to give the place an aged look. The furnishings were all in the Southwest vein. Overstuffed leather couches and chairs. There were wooden sideboards against the walls, including one in the dining room behind the vintage table and chairs. The one in the living room behind the seating area had been turned into a bar. There were assorted clay pots around to add to the ambiance and, of course, there were personal possessions—mementos and such—and family photographs dating back many decades covered the walls.

Leo and Ron were at the bar getting everyone drinks, while Kathy and Suzy were in the kitchen fixing the snacks we had brought with us. I joined Leo and Ron as Jacquie went to join Kathy and Suzy.

"Did you find everything?" I asked.

"Yes," Leo said as he handed me a cold one. "Everything is right where we left it last weekend."

"What do you think of the place, Ron?" I asked.

"This place is awesome," he said. "It's no wonder why Jacquie was raving about it when she told Kathy where we were going for the weekend. Where did you get that great painting on the wall there?"

It was a rather simple painting actually. It was a portrait of a beautiful brown stallion on a yellow field with various shading in the background. According to family legend, I told them, it was Grandpa Harry's own horse back in the day. It was painted by an old "desert rat" friend of his, simply because he loved the horse.

Whether that was true or not we'll never know. However, I remember seeing an old black-and-white photo of that horse standing in a pasture, and I always felt that if one had the photo colorized, it would be a dead ringer for the painting.

"The old prospector ended up selling it to Grandpa. I've heard his stuff is worth big bucks nowadays. I think it's perfect back there."

"So do I," said Leo lifting his beer in a toast. "To the old prospector."

"To the old prospector," Ron and I joined in.

"Whatever his name was," I laughed.

Meanwhile in the kitchen, Kathy said, "I want a kitchen like this in my house. I just love the design."

"Well," Jacquie said, "since you and Ron are looking for a house, try to find one in this old style."

"That won't be easy," Kathy said. "They don't make tract houses anywhere near as nice as this. At least not in our price range."

"Maybe someday," Suzy said.

"To someday," they toasted.

If you could see the kitchen, you'd know why Kathy was so impressed. It had a stove top built into an island in the middle. Over the island was a pot rack with assorted cooking utensils hanging down. Of course, the refrigerator and built-in ovens were in the brownish color that was currently popular. The sink was a farmhouse type. There were two windows. One faced the entry portico, and the other faced outward toward the front of the house.

When the snacks and drinks were ready, everyone adjourned to the courtyard, seating themselves comfortably on an array of lounge chairs that circled the firepit. From there, one could watch the dancing flames or gaze out at the pool and beyond, to the magnificent Santa Rosa Mountains, and watch the sun go down.

And that is exactly what we did. Jacquie and I settled into one of the double lounge chairs, Ron and Kathy took another, and Suzy and Leo took the singles. We all had blankets to cut the evening chill. We put a little music on the stereo and relaxed.

Leo had taken the chair closest to Suzy and had started a conversation. Jacquie noticed right away and gave me a little rib nudge as she gestured in their direction. I just smiled and said, "Maybe someone else will get lucky this weekend."

"You're so bad," she said, giving me another jab. Then she smiled and said, "From the looks of things, you might be right."

Just then we saw Leo steal a kiss.

"Looks like fun," I said. "Shall we?"

"Works for me," she said as she leaned in and got me in a lip-lock.

As the evening wound down, Ron and Kathy were the first to excuse themselves and adjourn to their bedroom. When Suzy made her exit, I think Leo may have joined her, because he left shortly after she did. That left Jacquie and me, curled up on our lounge chair. The only lights were the dying embers of the fire, the blue glow of the swimming pool light, and the full moon and stars. Being out away from the city lights, the sky was full of stars and the moon was big and bright. Jacquie and I cuddled very close in our lounge chair, and that is the way we woke up the next morning, still cuddled in each other's arms.

The morning sunlight woke us around seven. Most everyone else was already up. Jacquie and I were on our way to the kitchen to join the others. Just at that moment, Ray Ricco and Debbie Long arrived, escorted by Max through the front door. As much as we fully expected the two of them to cooperate with us by this point—after all, what choice did they have—Pop confided that Ray and Debbie were a couple of scared rabbits who might take off running in panic at any moment. So Pop instructed Max to tag along and keep an eye on them.

"Hi, Max," I said, barely acknowledging the other two. Then I said to the rest of the group gathered in the kitchen, "Good Morning, everyone."

"Nice of you two to join us," Leo said. "Did you have a nice night?"

I just gave him that "Uh, huh" look and said, "Yes, and *you*?"

He just gave me a smile and said, "As a matter of fact we did," and changed the subject.

Then to all of us he said, "We were just trying to decide what to do about breakfast. Since no one wants to cook, we decided to go into the Springs. Besides, the ladies want to do some power shopping. Any suggestions?"

When nobody spoke up, I said, "Well, I'm kind of partial to the Country Kitchen. Their waffles are fantastic. They've been written up in a lot of magazines and been around forever."

"I second that," Jacquie said. "My family went there all the time when we were little. I love the place."

"Sounds good to me," Ron said.

"I agree," Kathy said. "I love the place too."

"Okay," I said, looking at all the others. "Since there don't seem to be any objections, the Country Kitchen it is."

Everyone agreed. Except Ray and Debbie.

"We'd like to chill here," Ray said.

"Okay," I said. "I guess you can find something to snack on here."

"However, now we have a little problem," I said. "Who's going to watch those two?" I pointed at Ray and Debbie. Then I looked at Max. "Can't ask you to stay, even though that's why you're here. Do you think they can be trusted?"

"I think so," Max said, holding up his car keys. "I drove and without these, there is pretty much no place for them to go. Besides I need a break from these two, at least 'til after I've had my breakfast. I don't know how you've put up with them this long."

"Yeah," I said with a smile. "They've been a royal pain in the ass from the moment I met them. And we are kind of far from everything. I guess we can trust them. Besides, they're safer here than walking around on the street, and if they wish to remain included in our upcoming expedition, they're going to have to behave themselves and they know it." Then I said, looking them right in the eyes, "Okay, you can stay here by yourself. Just remember, you try anything that will get you on my wrong side, you're toast. Got it?"

"Yes," they both said sheepishly.

With that, we piled into our cars and headed downtown. After a great breakfast, Max decided to head back to the Hideaway for a nap and to keep an eye on his charges. The ladies left to do their shopping. The only thing they needed us guys for was to be the pack mules. After a full morning of going from store to store, the ladies decided to break for lunch.

"What a great idea," I said.

"Yeah," Ron and Leo chimed in.

"Don't give me that." Jacquie smirked and looked right at me. "We know you guys are tired of following us around all morning. Let's put this stuff in the car and go get a drink somewhere."

"*Yes,*" I said, pumping a fist.

"Don't act too happy," Jacquie said, smiling. "We can always go back to shopping."

"Oh, no, anything you want is all right with us. Right fellas?"

"Yes," they responded enthusiastically.

"That's more like it." Jacquie laughed as she was joined by the other ladies. "We want Mexican. Is that all right with you guys?"

"Mexican it is," I said with a smile. The guys just nodded in agreement.

We decided on Las Casuelas—it had been part of the Palm Springs scene since 1958. It had everything you could want. Atmosphere, great food, and even better drinks. Their margaritas were allegedly the best in town. I've had some pretty good margaritas in my time, so I thought to myself, *I'll be the judge of that.*

They were damn good.

Since the ladies had left all of their swag in the car, I asked, "So what all did you buy? It was certainly heavy enough."

"Wouldn't you like to know," Jacquie said. "Besides, the only reason we brought you guys along was to tote our stuff around."

"I knew it. They only want us for our bodies," I said with a smile.

"You got that straight," Jacquie responded, getting an enthusiastic thumbs up from Suzy and Kathy.

Ron, Leo, and I just shook our heads and laughed.

"Very funny. Since yours was the heaviest, can I inquire as to what you bought?" I asked Jacquie.

"Well, I hope you don't mind, but it's for you," she said.

"Aw, you shouldn't have," I said.

"But I have a little confession," she said. "It isn't just for you."

"Huh?" I said, looking at her quizzically.

Everyone else was quiet, as if mesmerized by this inside story they were getting. I felt a tiny bit uncomfortable but, well, I guessed that was just me.

"Well, it's actually for your apartment. It's something we both can enjoy," she said.

"Okay, I'm hooked," I said. "Now I really want to know what it is."

"It's a piece of Indian pottery. I saw it and thought it was lovely . . . that it would look great on your balcony with some flowers in it."

"I *thought* that box was a little heavy. Thank you," I said. "And you know, I think you should have something that reflects you in my place—a little bit of you and your style. I can't wait to see it."

"I'm so glad you feel that way. I was a little worried what you might think; like I'm pushing you into something you're not ready for," she said, looking relieved.

Everyone was *really* quiet now.

"Look, I love these guys"—I gestured at the rest of our group—"but I really don't want to discuss our relationship with them, at least not yet. So let me say just this. You're not pushing me into any situation I don't want to be in. We'll discuss the rest later," I said, trying to give her my warmest smile.

"All right," Kathy said, giving Jacquie a thumbs up.

"That goes double for me," Suzy said, giving another thumbs up.

"That goes for me too," Leo said.

"Ditto," Ron said.

"Thanks everybody. Here's to Indian pottery," I said, laughing as I raised my margarita in a toast.

"To pottery and everything it stands for," Leo said as everyone raised their drinks.

We all had a great lunch and a few more margaritas, then headed back to the Hideaway to soak up some sun and do a little swimming.

Mom, Pop, my sister Kay, and her husband Joe had arrived by the time we returned. They told us that they had invited Jacquie's dad, Jack, over for dinner. I guessed that this would be the night Suzy and Jacquie would find out they were sisters, and it was all I could do to keep from spilling the beans to Jacquie. I just hoped she wouldn't be too angry with me. However this would go, I was pretty sure we were in for an interesting evening.

CHAPTER 19

D inner was scheduled for eight so it could be enjoyed out-
doors in the cool of the evening around the pool. Drinks
were served at seven. Mom and Pop had invited some other
friends to the buffet-style affair. We had quite a crowd. When
added to our original nine, Mom and Pop and Kay and Joe
brought us up to thirteen. With the two other couples and Jack,
we had eighteen. Lucky for us, Jack and the other two couples
weren't sleeping over.

When I had a chance, I pulled Mom, Pop, Kay, and Joe aside,
so that Jacquie and I could show them the little present she had
bought me.

"It's beautiful," Mom said, reaching out to touch it. "Frenchy,
you should get something like that for here."

As he looked around, Pop frowned and said, "Don't you think
we have enough pots and things already?"

"No," Mom said, "you can never have enough plants. Or pots for
them. Especially a beautiful one like this. Jacquie has excellent taste."

"Yes, she does," Kay said, looking at me with a wink and a smile.

Then she turned to Joe. "I think we should get one, maybe two, to put around our pool."

"Yeah, sure," Joe said a little hesitatingly.

I turned to Jacquie and said softly, "See what trouble you've caused?" I smiled and elbowed her gently.

Jacquie's dad arrived around 7:30 and I motioned to him as he came in to meet me over by the bar for a few minutes. I wanted to know if he had found the letter from Melanie.

He had, so I asked him, "When are you going to tell Suzy and Jacquie?"

"I don't know," he said. "If I tell them now, that might spoil dinner, or I could wait until after we eat and tell them then."

I thought about it and said with a smile, "Maybe after dinner would be better. Then if they kill you, it won't spoil our meal."

He gave me a reluctant and sarcastic "heh, heh" and agreed that after dinner was probably best.

We returned to the guests and had a before-dinner drink or two. Poor ol' Jack's excuse was he'd need the fortification for what was going to happen after dinner. I was just drinking for the hell of it.

The dinner was very pleasant, nothing fancy. Pop grilled some steaks. They had brought a big bowl of potato salad from home and there was a big pot of baked beans. Perfect desert fare.

After dinner, I saw Jack up at the bar. He was having a couple more drinks for courage. Leo was tending bar. I walked up and said to Leo, "Shoot me a Corona, please."

"Thanks, and can Jack and I have a little privacy for a minute?" I said when he handed me my beer.

"Sure thing," he said as he gave the bar a swipe with the bar cloth, then left to join Suzy and Jacquie outside by the pool.

"Well, are you ready?" I asked Jack.

"Ready as I'll ever be," he said. He hesitated for a moment then said, "I'd like you to do me a solid."

"Okay," I said looking at him quizzically.

"I've decided to tell both Jacquie and Suzy at the same time, and I want you to be there, like . . . as backup," he said.

"Are you sure that's a good idea?" I asked.

"Yeah," he said. "I'm not sure how they'll react, and hell, I'm not sure how I'd react if someone dropped this on me. I need moral support."

"Okay, I can handle it if you can," I said. "Why don't we go into Pop's office—we'll have more privacy in there. I'll go get Jacquie and Suzy and meet you in there."

"Thanks, I owe you big," he said as he crossed himself and headed toward the office.

"Yes, you do, and I saw that. You must be scared, you're not even Catholic," I said with a smile.

He just looked at me and shook his head, then headed toward the office. I crossed myself and turned to go get the girls.

"I saw that," he said, and we both laughed.

I found Jacquie and Suzy out by the pool. They were talking to Leo.

Jacquie said to me, "Leo was telling me that you wanted a little privacy so you could talk to my dad. What's that all about?"

Neither she nor Suzy had a clue what was about to be dropped on them. It had been really tough for me to not tell her, too. I could only imagine what their reactions were going to be. The more I thought about it, the more I didn't envy Jack's next few minutes—this was quite a bomb. I also knew Jacquie had a temper, just like her mother. I'd been on the receiving end of it a couple of times. If she didn't react well, poor old Jack was really in for it.

"You're about to find out," I said. "Your dad wants to talk to you and Suzy in Pop's office, and he wants me to be there. For emotional support."

I got a bewildered look from all three of them.

"Don't worry, it's nothing like that—no one is dying!" I said, seeing the worry in their faces. And, to Leo, "I'll fill you in later."

"Okay," he said, giving me that WTF look.

I got the same look from Jacquie and Suzy, and it did not feel good, let me tell you. "Just come with me," I told them. "It's nothing horrible—please try not to worry."

When we entered the office, Jack was sitting behind Pop's desk, his arms stiffly at his sides. He looked like he was about to give a serious speech. Which I guess he was. "Please close the door and sit down," he told us. "And make yourselves comfortable."

"*You* don't look very comfortable," I said, smiling and trying to lighten things up with a joke; I bombed. No one laughed, and no one said anything.

I closed the door and we all sat down. Everyone was quiet for a minute.

Jacquie spoke first. "What's this all about, Dad? Why all the secrecy?"

"I don't know exactly how to say this, so I'll just come out with it." He cleared his throat and folded his hands together. "Jacquie, I'd like to introduce you to your sister, Suzy. Well, your half-sister."

You could practically hear their jaws drop.

Jack then handed Suzy the letter he received from Melanie and said, "I received it from your mother a few years ago. It explains everything."

Then he turned to Jacquie. "You can read the letter when she's done, but to make a long story short . . . her mother and I had an affair while we were both stationed in London during the war.

I never knew I had gotten her pregnant, and that I had another daughter, until I got that letter."

"But that was years ago that you got the letter!" Jacquie objected. Suzy nodded grimly.

"I decided not to say anything to anybody because I didn't see any point."

"You didn't see the *point*?" Jacquie said. "Really?"

"Well, Ruby and I were already divorced so I didn't feel the need to tell her. Besides, I didn't even *know* your mother when I had the affair. As for you and your brothers, since I didn't expect you to ever meet Suzy, I thought, why rock the boat?"

Jacquie was obviously a little shaken. She sat in silence for a second then said, "You should have told us. We would have understood. I'm mad at you. Not because of Suzy, but because you didn't trust us enough to tell us."

"I'm sorry, I fucked up. Can you forgive me?"

"It won't be easy, but yes," she said with—surprisingly—a reasonably forgiving smile. And even a hug. "But only because I'm getting a sister out of the deal."

Jack then turned to Suzy. Tears stood in his eyes. "How about you?" he asked.

She'd had a few minutes to let it all sink in and didn't look terribly surprised. All she said was, "Hi, Dad. Hi, Sis."

Then he embraced them both at once. They stood there for some time, in this big hug.

I just wiped my brow and said, "Whew."

Jacquie heard me and gave me a dirty look. "You knew, didn't you? How long have you known and why didn't you tell me?"

"I've only known since yesterday at the Cove . . . I swear. When we introduced everyone to each other. As soon as I asked him if he remembered Suzy's mom from London, he spilled the beans. He asked me not to say anything to you or Suzy, because he wanted to tell you himself when he figured out how to do it. Also, he wanted time to find that letter. You don't know how hard it was for me not to tell you. I'm sorry."

"I forgive you," she said as she gave me a kiss. "But you'll pay— you owe me," she said, grinning.

"I can hardly wait," I said, smiling.

"Wow, this is amazing," Suzy said. "I now have a whole new family. How many brothers do you have?" she asked.

"Two," Jacquie said. "Jack Junior is the oldest and Jeff, he's my younger brother."

"Wow," she said again. "My real father, a sister, two brothers, and a brother-in-law."

"What was that?" I said.

"Silly goose." Suzy grinned. "All anybody has to do is look at you two. We all know it's going to happen—you just haven't figured it out yet," she said with a laugh and a smile.

"You and I need to talk," I said to Jacquie.

"Yes, we do," she said smiling.

Then Jack broke the tension and said, "I guess we're all done here. Let's rejoin the party."

"Copy that," I said. "I need to fill Leo in on what's going on before he bursts with curiosity."

Then I turned to Jacquie and said, "Later, babe."

"Copy that," she said with a smile.

"All done here," Suzy repeated dreamily, then laughed. "This really changes a lot of things in my life."

"Yes, it does, in mine too, and we need to tell Kathy," Jacquie said to Suzy. "Let's go—she'll never believe it."

"I guess I should go tell your old man too—he's probably wondering what's going on, and he deserves to know," Jack said to me.

"Definitely," I said.

When we were back outside, Jacquie went to look for Kathy, but Suzy stayed back a little. She placed a hand on my forearm to stop me.

"I didn't mean to embarrass you in there, with that whole 'I guess this makes you my new brother-in-law' thing," she said with a smile.

"That's okay," I said. "You just caught me by surprise. I didn't think it was that obvious that I'm falling for her."

"Well, it is and don't feel bad. The guy is usually the last one to know anyway," she said, starting to laugh.

I stood there blinking as she walked away, feeling like yes, part of me did know it. Then I started to laugh.

While Suzy went off to find Jacquie and Kathy, I went to find Leo, laughing all the way. I was sure he was dying of curiosity.

"Guess what?" I said when I found him.

"What's happening?" he asked with a little exasperation. "I've been dying over here."

"Jacquie and Suzy are sisters," I said.

"What?" he asked with that WTF look.

"That's right," I said. "Apparently Jack got a little when he was in London during the war, and Suzy's the result of that experience; she's his daughter."

"WOW. I'll be damned," he said. "I think that calls for a drink, don't you?"

"Absolutely," I said, and we headed for the bar.

The word soon spread to the entire gathering. Congratulations were offered all around. The ladies all got together to do their thing, while Pop invited all the male guests into the study for

Cuban cigars and imported brandy that he kept only for special occasions. We couldn't think of anything more special than this. When everybody's glass was full and the Cohibas were passed out and lit, we all raised our glasses in a toast.

"To Jack and his new daughter," Pop said.

"To Jack and his new daughter," we all responded with cheers as we clicked our snifters together.

Then I said to Pop, "Did you know about Jack and Melanie when you were all together in London?"

"I didn't have a clue. They obviously did a damn good job of keeping it quiet," he said. "When she told us she was pregnant and had to resign from the Royal Navy, I just took it for granted that her husband had knocked her up before leaving for the Pacific. As for Jack, he never gave it away that he and Melanie had anything going on."

"Well, it looks like they did," I said with a chuckle.

"It sure does," Pop concurred, as we clicked our glasses again.

"Great brandy," I said.

"Thanks," Pop said.

"These Cohibas are pretty good, too," I said. "You got to tell me where you get them."

"Trust me," he said with a chuckle, "you *don't* want to know."

"Maybe that's for the best," I said as I stood at attention and saluted.

Pop just smiled and returned the salute.

The brandy really was delicious and the cigars were great, and all things considered, the party was a smashing success. When things eventually broke up, and the mess was cleaned up, people started retiring to their respective rooms. Mom and Pop took one of the big rooms at the back of the building, and Kay and her husband Joe took the other one. Ray and Debbie went off to their room, leaving

Suzy, Leo, Ron, Kathy, Jacquie, and me lounging around the dying fire and gazing at another full moon. Ron and Kathy disappeared first, followed shortly thereafter by Suzy and Leo. By the looks of it, I thought, Jack might be gaining another son-in-law sooner than he might be anticipating.

I said to Jacquie, "Suzy and Leo are getting pretty close to each other. What does your female intuition tell you? You think they're going to be an item?"

"You never know—it does look like it's warming up a little," she said.

"Now," I said, "you heard her refer to me as her new brother-in-law. What's that all about?"

"That's right! She did, didn't she."

"Yes, she did. Does she know something I don't?" I asked teasingly.

"I have no idea what she's talking about," she said coyly. "I think I need to have a talk with her."

"You do that," I said with a devilish smile as I pulled her in close and gave her a deep kiss. We fell back onto the lounge chair as we had the night before. After some serious necking, we fell asleep in each other's arms once again. This was getting to be a pleasant habit, I thought to myself. Suzy just might be on to something.

Tomorrow was another day of lounging around the pool before getting back to the real world and our impending treasure hunt.

CHAPTER 20

Twenty-six miles across the sea,
Santa Catalina is a-waitin' for me.
Santa Catalina, the island of romance,
romance, romance, romance . . .

The sweet sound of one of my all-time favorites was wafting out of my car radio as I headed into work that Monday. A song that probably had the most influence on me to go to sea—it was without a doubt the inspiration for my very first real sailing adventure. Sailboats and girls, not necessarily in that order, are two of the things I love most in this world. My family had always had the boat, and now I had the girl.

Back when I was in my sophomore year in high school, my best friends, Larry, John, Charlie, and I decided to *borrow* the *Black Widow* for a little excursion to Catalina. Larry worked part-time as cleanup person at a local liquor store. We pooled our money, he put it in the cash register, and after closing, six cases of Budweiser magically appeared behind the dumpster in the parking lot. We all made our various excuses to our parents as to whose home we would be staying at that weekend. We loaded a little bit of food and a lot of beer aboard the *Black Widow* and sailed off to the Island of Romance.

Little did we know, the guy who ran the bait shop in Fleitz Brothers Marina was a friend of my dad's, and he kept an eye on the boat for my old man. When he noticed it was missing from its slip, and my dad hadn't told him he was going out, he called him. Pop then called a friend of his with the Coast Guard, and, by the evening, we were all in custody and the *Black Widow* was being towed back to its mooring.

We were all turned over to our respective parents. Pop put on a good show of being angry, but down deep inside, I knew he felt a little admiration for my Tom Sawyer-esque escapade. I was duly grounded for a month, and told that next time, forget the beer and just ask if I wanted to borrow the boat. I've been asking ever since, but nowadays, we both know we never forget the beer.

Nevertheless, since my first failed attempt at piracy, the sea has been in my blood. Now we were about to take the adventure to a new level. When I got to work, my dad called and said Uncle Jack got the diving permit. The treasure hunt was on. Since we had already asked Leo and my brother-in-law Joe to join us, I only needed one more to round out our crew. I called Marco to see if he was available. Fortunately, he was, so I filled him in on the caper. All he said was, "I'm in." With Pop and Uncle Jack tagging along, that made six, and we were ready to go. As I said, my brother-in-law was an LA City fireman, and his duty station just happened to be on the fireboat in the harbor—one of his duties was to act as a diver for the department. Plus, Joe possessed a range of highly practical skills and get-er-done know-how that all big city firefighters are taught in their rigorous training programs.

We needed at least two of us who could dive for our little expedition; I was the other guy with the required experience. I had one more call to make before getting down to work. I called Captain Pete's dive shop.

"Cap'n Pete's Saloon and Dive Shop, get wet on the inside and on the outside. Pete speaking," he said when he answered. You could tell he'd answered exactly that way a gazillion times. You could also tell that after all the years, he was tired of repeating it.

"I'd like to do both, this afternoon," I said and chuckled. "How you doin'? This is Kit O'Banion. Have you got our equipment ready? The dive is on for this coming weekend, so I'm just checkin' in."

"Hi, yourself. Yeah, it's all ready to go," he said.

"Good," I said. "I'll be down to pick it up after work today. Say around five. I have to go get the Bronco first."

"No problem," he said. "I'll be more than happy to have Gus, my assistant, drive it down and put it on your boat."

"That would be more convenient," I said, relieved to take one item off my mental checklist. "You do know where Pop keeps it?"

"Sure do," he said. "Down at Fleitz Brothers. Been down there lots of times."

"Cool," I said. "That will save me a trip. I wasn't looking forward to the traffic down to Manhattan Beach and back during rush hour. Thanks."

"No problem," he said again and hung up.

That was one less thing I had to do today. I decided to call Pop back and give him an update.

"Triangle Investigations, Jacquie speaking. How may I help you?" the lovely voice answered.

"I can think of a million ways," I said with a slight laugh. "But unfortunately, this is business. Is Pop available?"

She just giggled, and said, "Aw, I wanted to hear more about those million ways. Hold on—I'll get him."

"That won't be necessary," said Pop, who must have just stuck his head through the door.

"It's Kit," she said.

"That's good—I wouldn't want you to talk to all of our clients that way," he said jovially. "I'll take it in my office."

"I heard that," I said, chuckling. "And Jacquie . . . we can discuss those million ways later."

"Yes, later would be better," Pop said as he picked up the phone in his office. You could hear the smile in his voice.

"I'll hang up now," Jacquie said, laughing.

"Yes, now would be nice," Pop said as he started to laugh.

Then the laughter subsided, and it was only me and Pop on the line.

Pop asked, "Okay, what's up?"

"I just called to give you an update," I said, still trying to stifle my laughter. "Called Captain Pete, he's going to drop the gear off at the *Widow*, that will save me a trip down and back at rush hour. Also, I've rounded out our crew with Marco."

"Good," he said. "Marco is a good man. Very dependable."

"So, I guess we're ready," I said.

"You sound a little worried," Pop said. "What's eating you?"

"Captain Pete," I said. "Don't get me wrong, I like the old guy. After all, we've been friends and patrons of his for a long time. I know he, you, and Uncle Jack go way back. It's just the way he played Tony Cornero back in the day and was going to play Ray and Debbie. I just don't know if we can trust him anymore."

"You've got to trust your gut. It never lies," Pop said. "*But*, I think we can handle him if he tries to pull anything."

"I suppose you're right," I said. "Just precombat jitters."

"That's all it is," he said. "Just shake it off."

Then he changed the subject.

"I've arranged to have all our food and drinks to be delivered to the boat. The bait shop is handling that. You've got Pete delivering the gear. It looks like we're all set. Has everyone arranged to get the three-day weekend?" Pop asked.

"Joe has rearranged his schedule at the fire department. Leo, Marco, and I are taking care of that today, now that we know it's on," I said.

"Good, then I guess we're done. Call me if anything comes up, otherwise I'll see you Friday night. Do you want me to transfer you back to Jacquie?" he asked.

"As much as I'd love you to, I have to get to work. Just tell her I love her, and I'll talk to her later."

"I think she knows that, but I'll tell her anyway. Catch you later."

Everything was set. I had to work Friday, but Leo and Marco arranged to get a four-day weekend, and Joe could trade shifts, so he was able to get four days off in a row, too. We would take off Friday night and be off of San Nicholas by dawn.

CHAPTER 21

had settled in for the day's business. Around two, Jacquie called.

"Nick is going to be with my mom tonight. You want to get together for dinner?" she asked.

"Yeah," I said. "How would you like to try some seafood?"

"Perfect."

"Kay's friend Ladean is waitressing at a new seafood joint in Glendale called Clancy's. She says the food is great."

"Sounds great," she said. "I'll be getting off early, so how about you pick me up at my place around five?"

"Great. See you then, and dress casual—it's a jeans and T-shirt kinda place. Love you."

"Back at you," she said and hung up.

At five sharp, I pulled up in front of her building. I noticed a lot of Sheriff's vehicles around. When I got inside Jacquie's apartment, I asked her what all the activity was for.

"Oh," she said. "That's the Sheriff's mounted posse. They keep their horses in that stable across the street. They practice their maneuvers here in the early morning hours so they can be in the street without disrupting traffic. They march right in front of my apartment window."

"That must be neat," I said. "Does the noise bother you?"

"No, it's actually quite restful," she said. "I like to sit on my balcony and watch them parade by. Sometimes I even lie in bed with the window open and just listen to the sounds of the horses. It helps me fall asleep."

"That sounds nice," I said. "Do you ever listen to music while you're watching the parade?"

"Actually, I have," she said. "I got a copy of Ravel's *Bolero*. If you time it just right, just as the song hits its crescendo, the horses are right out in front of my apartment."

"Neat," I said. "I've always liked *Bolero*—it's one of my favorites."

"Wow, you know it?"

"Yes—does that surprise you?"

"No, I mean . . . Well, maybe you'll have to join me some evening and we can enjoy it together," she said with a smile.

"I'm looking forward to it," I said with a big grin on my face.

With that we went to dinner.

Clancy's was relatively new, open only a few months. It was a funky place with sawdust on the floor, benches for seats, checkered tablecloths, and such. Ladean was on duty tonight. She was easy to spot, wearing a baseball cap with her dark brown hair ponytailed through the back of it, and an apron with Clancy's logo on it. She saw us as we walked in and motioned to us to come over to a nice booth in the corner.

"Hi, guys," she said. "I'll be your waitress. You must be Jacquie—I'm Ladean. I've heard so much about you." She said all this very quickly, before I could introduce her.

"Oh!" Jacquie said, giving me a quizzical look.

I just shrugged.

"Yes, Kit's sister Kay has told me all about you," she said. "She thinks you're just wonderful."

"*Oh!*" both Jacquie and I said, as I gave her an "and now I understand" look.

Kay had known Jacquie as long as I had. She had watched Jacquie grow up just as I did. Among my sister's many endearing qualities—or annoying ones, depending on your perspective—is that she loved to gossip. If you don't want anyone to know your business, don't ever confide in my sister. I love her very much, but there are times, like right then, that I'd like to have a word with her.

"Well, that's very nice of you to pass on—thank you," Jacquie said, looking at me trying to figure out what was going on.

"I'll tell you later," I whispered, as we crawled into the booth and picked up our menus.

"Would you like something to drink while you look at those?" Ladean asked.

"Sure, but first . . . what do you recommend?" I asked.

"It's all good," she said. "But I think you'll enjoy the snapper. It's great."

"Um, the snapper sounds great. I'll have that and a glass of Merlot," Jacquie said.

"One red snapper and a Merlot coming up," Ladean said. "And you?" she asked me.

"I'll have the fried oysters and a Corona," I said.

"Great, that is one red snapper and a Merlot for the lady and oysters and a Corona for the gentleman. I'll put your order in and be right back with your drinks," she said.

As soon as she was out of earshot, Jacquie asked, "Okay, what's the deal. She's heard about me, but I haven't heard about her?"

"You heard her. This is all on Kay. Sort of," I said.

"*Sort of?*" she asked, sarcastically.

"Look, I don't know how she found out, but I think Mom let it slip that we got back together down in La Quinta, and she's been bugging me about it ever since," I said. "And of course there was the family gathering last weekend down in La Quinta."

"Did she know what your dad had in mind about hiring me?" she asked.

"I don't think so, but when you showed up here, I think she put two and two together and took it from there," I said. "But the only friends I've told about you are Kathy, Leo, and my buddy Marco. I haven't seen anybody else to tell. Besides, I don't go around broadcasting my personal life to everyone I meet. I take our relationship seriously, and it's nobody else's business. As for Kay, she loves to run her mouth off. We have a little joke in our family. 'Tell Kay, tell the world.'"

"And you've never called her out on this?"

"Does no good. She couldn't keep a secret if her life depended on it. I love her but I don't tell her anything. If she ever asks you why I never confide in her, now you know. I learned my lesson a *long* time ago."

"What did she do?" she asked.

"Aside from this?" I asked with a tone of sarcasm. "It wasn't anything specific, it just seems that every time I confide in her, even the most insignificant little thing, somebody is asking about it within twenty-four hours. And I do mean every time. I never mentioned La Quinta, much less running into you again, precisely because of this."

"I didn't know. She never showed that side to me," Jacquie said. "She gave me tennis lessons when I was in high school. We always got along fabulously."

"Yes, but did you ever her tell her anything really personal?"

"No," she said.

"And you didn't have any mutual friends either, did you?" I asked.

"Oh. That's true. Now I think I understand," she said.

Just then, Ladean arrived tableside with our drinks. "Your dinner will be along soon," she said, then she asked, "Are you two going by Fremont Park tonight to watch Kay play in the tennis tournament?"

"I don't know," Jacquie said. I couldn't help but hear a tiny bit of annoyance in her voice at Ladean's sudden familiarity with her, and I couldn't quite blame her. Ladean didn't wait for an answer—also one of her signature traits.

"Well, if you are," she barreled on, "I'll see you there. You two are my last customers for tonight and I'll be heading over to watch it."

"I hadn't thought about it," I said. "Would you like to go?" I asked Jacquie. "It will end fairly early, since this is Monday."

"Yes, sounds like fun," she said.

Then she said to Ladean, "I know she's good, she gave me tennis lessons back when I was in high school."

"I know," Ladean said. "She told me all about it."

I started to smirk and gave Jacquie an *I told you so* look. Jacquie just nodded.

Yeah," I said, "she's been playing ever since she was little. She taught me how to play, but no matter how good I got, she was always better. It's embarrassing to be beaten by your sister all the time," I laughed.

"It's okay, Bucky. I'm sure there are other things that you are better at than her," Jacquie said with a wink.

I just smiled and said, "Uh huh. Maybe later you could elaborate?"

"I'd love to," Jacquie said.

"I think I'll leave you two alone and go get your food," Ladean said with a smile.

"Thanks," Jacquie and I said.

When Ladean was gone, I asked Jacquie, "Are you angry with Kay?"

"No," she said. "I understand. I didn't have a sister growing up, just two brothers. Kay kinda filled that gap in many ways. And now she really is becoming family. Of course I forgive her."

When we got to the courts at Fremont Park, we found Joe in the stands watching the matches. Kay was already playing. Jacquie sat down next to him.

"Make yourself comfortable," I said to her. "I'm going to see Rolle and get us some drinks. Would you like a Coke?"

"That would be great," she said.

"Do you want anything?" I asked Joe.

"Sure, I'll have a Corona," he said.

"A Corona?" Jacquie asked me with a surprised look. "This is a public park—where are you going to get beer? Do you have to go back to that liquor store we passed? And who's Rolle?"

"Not to worry," I said. "I don't have to go any farther than the parking lot. Rolle has everything you could want to drink in the trunk of his car. It's his little side deal. He picks up a few extra bucks and everybody can drink whatever they want."

"In that case, change mine to a Merlot, if he's got it," she said with a smile.

"One Merlot and two Coronas coming up," I said as I gave her a little peck on the cheek and went to fetch our drinks.

By the time I returned with our beverages in hand, Ladean had arrived, having finished her work shift, and she and Joe were in the midst of introducing Jacquie to some of the other tennis people. So I just distributed our drinks and settled in with the rest of these folks to watch Kay play her match, which she won with no problem. The matches finally broke up around eleven, and since we all had to work the next day, we headed home.

When we arrived back at Jacquie's place, the Sheriff's posse had assembled about a half mile from the front of her apartment building and were getting ready to start their maneuvers.

"Do you want to stay?" Jacquie asked. "I have some of your Czech Michelob. I can put on *Bolero* and we can watch the show."

"You don't know how tempting that is. But I think I've already drunk too much. Besides, if I want to be functional tomorrow, I'd better not stay," I said, pulling her in closely to give her a good-night kiss.

"Okay. If you insist," she said as she closed in for another even more passionate embrace.

"Be strong. Resist," I muttered to myself. As much as I wanted to stay, I let her go to bed by herself, and headed home. I managed to see her a couple more times that week, but soon it was Friday. The expedition would commence.

CHAPTER 22

I got off at three that afternoon. I had brought a change of clothes with me so I could head straight to the boat. Pop, Uncle Jack, and Joe were already there making final preparations to get underway. Marco and Leo arrived shortly after I did.

"Hi, guys," I said as they walked up. "Hand me your gear and I'll stow it below. You guys ready for some adventure?"

"You got that straight," Marco said. "Permission to come aboard?"

"Permission granted," I said. They knew the drill.

Just then Pop, Uncle Jack, and Joe returned from the bait shop, weighted down with loads of goodies.

"Let me give you a hand," Leo said.

"Thanks," Pop said. "You both know Jack?"

"Yeah," they acknowledged. Everyone shook hands; the formalities thus dispensed with, we got down to business.

"Where's Max?" I said to Uncle Jack, adding teasingly, "You never go anywhere without him."

"He doesn't like boats, especially ones on the ocean. So, I gave him the weekend off," Jack said. "Besides, he has a girlfriend you know, and he made it very clear he'd prefer to spend the weekend with her rather than with us."

"Makes perfect sense to me. As much as I love sailing, I can think of somewhere else I'd rather be this weekend," I said with a grin.

"I know," he said. "She is a wonderful lady and a great addition to the company."

"Copy that," I said.

Then Pop said, "It's about 1700 hours now, for you landlubbers that's 5:00 p.m. By the time we get out of here and hit the channel, it's going to be dark. We'll motor over. We should be off San Nicholas in the morning. Once we're out on the water, Kit and I will take the first watch while the rest of you get some sleep. Joe and Leo will take the second."

"Aye, captain," we all said with mock salutes.

"You guys are too funny," Pop said, shaking his head, but nevertheless returning the salute.

After all our personal gear was stowed, we cast off and headed out of the harbor. The diving gear was aboard the boat just as Captain Pete had promised. It was a good distance from San Pedro where we were docked to San Nicholas Island. A heavy marine layer was headed in. Though we were sailing under power, in the fog it would be a slow go.

———

We had been underway about four hours and were about midway to the island when conditions worsened. The fog was so thick you could only see a few feet in any direction. We had all been so stoked about the upcoming dive that nobody could sleep, so the beer had been broken open about two hours earlier and, by this time, none of us were feeling any pain. Leo had even brought out a joint that was being passed around. Needless to say, we were rather oblivious to the heavy fog. Not a good situation considering what happened next.

All of a sudden, the engine started to sputter and then it stopped. We popped the engine hatch cover, and Joe, being the most familiar with boat engines, grabbed a flashlight and leaned in to take a look.

"Not good," he said. "Someone's been fooling around with the fuel lines and the cooling system. We've been sabotaged."

"What?" Pop said. "Impossible. She was running just fine. Nobody's been aboard but us!"

"Not true," I said. "Gus and Captain Pete were aboard. They delivered all the diving equipment."

"*That son of a bitch!*" Pop bellowed. "Wait till I get my hands on him. You were right, Kit—we shouldn't have trusted him."

"You got that straight," Uncle Jack said. "I should've known, especially considering his involvement in the original heist."

"I'll deal with Captain Pete personally," Pop raged. "He sabotaged my baby. He's going to pay."

"Can you get us going?" I asked Joe.

"I think so, but it'll only be temporary. This baby is going to have to go into the shop when we get back," Joe said. "It's going to take a while so you guys might as well chill while I go to work."

Pop was furious. "Get to it, I guess," he said. "I'm going to *kill* that bastard when I see him."

"I think he's pissed," I whispered to Leo as I took the joint from him. "I think Pop needs this more than you."

"Here Pop, this might help a little," I said as I handed him the joint.

"Thanks," he said as he smiled and took a hit. "I do need that."

So, there we were, dead in the water in the middle of the shipping lane. Small, rippling waves slapped gently at the sides of the boat. Somewhere far off, a gull called. Since there was room for only one to work in the tight space of the engine compartment, the rest of us each had another beer, as Leo lit and passed around another J. It wasn't long before we were all mesmerized by the rocking of the boat and Joe in the hold, clanking away, working on fixing the engine. I offered him a toke, but he declined, since he was so close to the fuel line. Thank god he had his head on straight at that point.

"When I'm all done," he said, nodding at the smoking joint in my hand. I took a peek over his shoulder, saw the tools and engine parts arrayed before him. Internal combustion engines were not my forte, be they marine or auto, so it was all over my head. I just said, "Far out, man."

Then Marco said, "This is cool, man."

Then Leo said, "Yeah, dude. Far out."

Pop looked at us like we were crazy. Then he took another a hit.

"Far out," he said, and these many minutes after his fury with Captain Pete, Pop seemed like he was finally cool.

About an hour and another joint later, Joe was just about finished. It was even foggier that it had been before, if that was even possible. I could feel the microdroplets of moisture on my face; it was cold and clammy. The water seemed to be getting a little choppier, the waves hitting the sides of the boat not so gentle anymore.

Then, out of nowhere came the earsplitting blast of a ship's horn!

You wanna talk about a bunch of stoned guys, their eyes popping out of their heads like thyroid cases, hearts instantly pounding out of our chests, ears perked, staring at each other like a pack of prairie dogs hearing the roar of a mountain lion? Well, that was us.

Then—sliding like a silent avalanche out of the fog—the running lights of the biggest fucking tanker any of us had ever seen! It was bearing right down on us!

"Hurry it up, Joe! We've got company!" I yelled.

"I'm going as fast as I can!" he yelled back.

By this time, we were bouncing around like a cork in a bathtub from the surge the tanker pushed in front of it. It couldn't have been more than ten or twenty feet away when we all heard the sweet sound of the engine turning over. At the helm, Pop shoved it into gear and the *Widow* practically jumped away from the tanker as it sailed passed our stern, missing us by barely a hair. The whole thing was very surreal considering our mental state.

"*Far out!*" we all said in unison.

One more tale to tell our grandkids, if we ever lived long enough to have any.

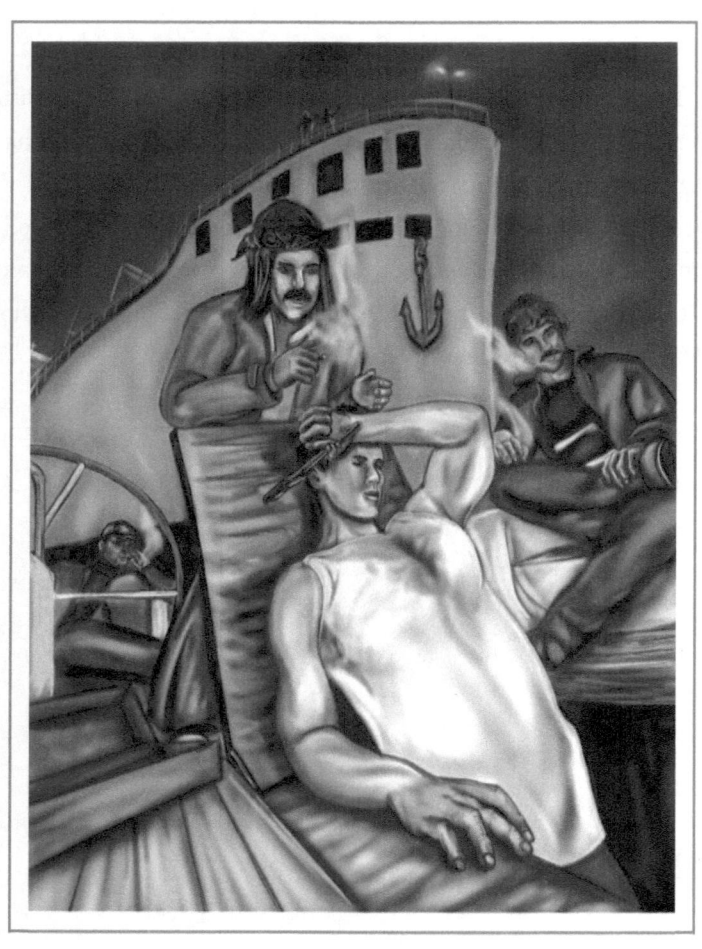

Just missed us. FAR OUT!

CHAPTER 23

We arrived at our rendezvous point around dawn. There had been no further incidents and we were sober enough for the day's upcoming events. Pop dropped the *Widow*'s anchor and settled in to wait for Captain Pete to arrive. We could hardly wait to see what Pop was going to really do to Captain Pete; we knew he wouldn't really kill him of course, even though he was angry enough to give that some serious thought, but we knew he would do something *big*. After a brief breakfast, Joe and I suited up and went over the side for a practice dive. Leo, Marco, Pop, and Uncle Jack stayed aboard.

After about an hour, I motioned to Joe to go up and he nodded in agreement. Just as we were about to hit the surface, I noticed there was another boat tied up next to ours. I assumed it was Pete. We came up under the dive platform. That was as good a place as any to get out of the water.

As I hoisted myself aboard the platform, I saw the name painted on the stern of the boat. It was the *Offshore Flo*, Captain Pete's dive boat. We heard some shouting from the cockpit of the *Black Widow*. I assumed it was Pop giving it to Captain Pete.

I whispered to Joe, "I wish I could hear what Pop is saying. It sounds like Pop's laying into Pete really good."

"Copy that," Joe said.

Since Joe and I had taken a couple of spear guns with us on our dive in case of sharks, we unloaded our dive gear, grabbed our spear guns, and headed slowly and quietly forward to see what was going on. What we saw came as a complete shock.

Captain Pete and Gus, Pete's deckhand, were standing with their backs to us and they had pistols pointed at Pop, Uncle Jack, Marco, and Leo.

This was an interesting predicament.

Pop saw me out of the corner of his eye and nodded slightly. I pointed my spear gun at the middle of the captain's back, and Joe did the same with Gus.

"Lay your weapons gently on the deck and don't try anything funny, or you'll have a spear coming out of your chest where your heart used to be," I demanded.

Then, in my best *Dirty Harry* impersonation, I said, "Unless you're feeling lucky. Are you feeling lucky, boys? Go ahead—make my day."

They didn't laugh. But they did lay down their guns. Pop gathered them up quickly and covered Gus and Pete while Joe and I quickly slipped out of our wet suits. I then moved around to the front of the boat, took one of the pistols from Pop, and sat down comfortably so that we could all have a nice little chat.

"I'm glad you guys showed up," Pop said. "The captain and I were having a little discussion about my severed gas line."

"All right, spill it," I said to Pete. "I don't think I need to ask why you were holding these guys at gunpoint?"

"Just a little renegotiation," the captain said. "I thought we could beat you to it, but you got here ahead of us."

"Then it was you who sabotaged our fuel line," I said.

"Yeah," he said, "but it didn't slow you down enough, it seems."

"You prick, you almost got us killed. We came this close," I said, holding up the thumb and finger of my free hand, "to getting sliced in half by a tanker. I oughta shoot you right now; chalk it up to carrying out the law of the sea dealing with scumbag saboteurs."

"Don't be too hasty," he said, holding both palms up. "Kill me and you'll never find what you are looking for."

"Tell me more," I said.

"As I told you back at the dive shop, the gold is buried on the island over there. In a cave."

"Okay," I said. "But we already know that. So where exactly is this little cave you're talking about?"

He pointed over to the northern tip of San Nicholas.

"See those two rocks out there? There is a little cove behind them. In the middle of the cove shore are two more smaller rocks. The entrance to the cave is between those rocks. About twenty feet down."

"Well, well," I said. "It looks like Joe and I are going to be making another dive shortly. You and Gus will stay here with Uncle Jack and Pop. Leo and Marco will come with us, and we're borrowing the *Flo*. We don't want to risk the *Widow* trying to get past those rocks, especially with a bad fuel line. If the engine craps out while we're going past the rocks, we're fucked."

"*No*, if you take the *Flo*, I'm coming with you," Captain Pete protested.

"The hell you are," I said flashing the pistol. "You're in no position to argue right now. Hey, Pop, you still have some cuffs aboard, don't you?"

"As a matter of fact, I do," he said, a wry smile on his face. "You know me—always prepared."

"Good. Cuff 'em, Danno," I said to Pop. "While you and Uncle Jack keep these birds company, Leo and Marco will maneuver the boat while we make our dive."

"Copy that. Oh, one more thing, Pete," Pop said.

"What?" he said, turning to look at Pop with a glum look.

"This!" he said as he gave him a quick right to the jaw. "That's for the tanker."

"Way to go, Pop," I said as everybody but Gus cheered. We knew Pop would pay Captain Pete back for what he'd done, we just didn't know how. All I can say is, it was great when the moment came.

We went back aboard the *Offshore Flo* and motored over to the cove. Joe was steering, and he decided to enter the cove through the little passageway between the southernmost rock and the shore. Leo, Marco, and I objected, but it was too late. We were—for better or for worse—committed.

Threading that boat through that narrow passageway was like trying to surf the Banzai Pipeline. Several times, the sides of the boat struck rock. We all held our breaths, scraping along like that, and I think we all secretly wanted to kill Joe; that is, until we finally got through. So instead, we all just looked at each other in relief, shook our heads, and I declared, "Far out!"

We dropped our hook about ten yards off the entrance to the cave. Leo and Marco stayed aboard per our plan, while Joe and I made our dive. I have to admit, knowing the growing list of antics that Captain Pete was pulling, I was rather surprised that we found the entrance right where the captain said it would be. It was a beautiful grotto. It was well lit by sunlight that filtered down through the rocks from above.

At the rear of the grotto was a small beach. We came out of the water there.

"WOW," I said, as we got out of the water to remove our tanks and masks. "I wish I had Pop's underwater camera. This is beautiful."

"I know," Joe said. "And really, unless we go back to the *Widow* and get it now, we'll never get to see this again."

"That's a great idea," I said. "After we're done here, we'll go get it and come back for some pictures. Only this time we'll go around the seaward side of the rocks." I said it sarcastically, but I really meant it seriously.

"Roger that," he nodded.

According to Pete, the loot was buried on the beach, somewhere right about in the center. We had brought some shovels with us, the ones that Pete had aboard the *Flo* as per Pop's instructions and intended for just this purpose. We started our dig.

After a few minutes, we hit something.

"This is it!" we said in unison.

Sand was flying everywhere, then there it was. Not exactly what we were looking for, but a find nevertheless. There, in the shallow hole, were the bodies of two sailors. No tags or identifying info, but sailors all the same. Their skeletons were wearing decayed Navy dungarees, easily recognizable to anyone who had ever been in the Navy. Each of their skulls had what looked to be a .45 bullet hole right between the eyes.

"I'll bet these are two of Nick's ex-Navy guys, the ones he hired to assist him with the heist and cover-up," I said.

"You might be right," Joe said. "It looks like ol' Nick was up on his pirate lore—dead men do, in fact, tell no tales."

"Copy that," I said. "Another reason to come back with Pop's camera and get some pictures. Only this time, it won't be of the scenery."

When we were back aboard the *Flo*, we got out of our wet suits and grabbed a couple of Coronas.

"Well, what did you find?" Leo asked.

"You'd be surprised," I said, then filled him and Marco in on the situation.

"Crap," Leo said.

"I'll second that!" Marco said, showing his frustration. "All of this for nothing."

"Not for nothing," I said. "We've answered a few questions. I think this explains how Nick Colleti came up with the bucks to buy his own casino in Vegas. Uncle Jack's going to love this."

"Well, now what do we do?" Joe asked.

"There's nothing we can do now," I told him. "We'll go back and tell Pop. We're not even supposed to be on this island," I said. "If we tell the Navy these two are here, there will be questions. Lots of questions. Questions that could even get us a little stay as a guest of the Feds. No, we have to find another way to connect Nick to these guys and hopefully get him to confess. Pop will think of something. Then we can notify the Navy. In the meantime, Captain Pete has some more explaining to do."

We decided to try a different way out of the cove, one that wasn't so harrowing. If we had only gone around the rocks on the seaward side in the first place, we would have had a nice wide-open passage into the cove. But then again, we wouldn't have had the pleasure of putting some nice new scratches and dings in Captain Pete's boat.

When we tied up next to the *Black Widow*, we filled Pop and Uncle Jack in on the "scientific findings" of our research expedition.

"It looks like your buddy Nick fucked you, Captain Pete," I said, "but not anywhere near as bad as he fucked those two guys in the cave."

"What two guys?" Captain Pete asked.

"I'm guessing it's two of the Navy guys that he used to pull the heist. And I mean *used*. It would seem he retrieved the loot, screwing you out of your share, and left the two Navy guys with nothing but bullet holes in their skulls where their brains used to be. They've been there awhile. All that's left is their skeletons."

"I guess he didn't go to the East Coast boys to finance his casino after all," Uncle Jack interjected.

"So it would seem," I responded.

Then I said to Captain Pete, "I'm surprised you're still walking around. After all, Nick went to a lot of trouble to make sure nobody else came out here."

Pop said, "Okay, everyone, listen up. Our next move will be to contact Nick Colleti and confront him about all this. Maybe we can blackmail him into letting our friends Ricco and Debbie off the hook."

"It would be even better," I said, "if we could force him to cop to the two stiffs on the island. Then we would have a legitimate reason to notify the Navy that they're there and he should pay. They may have been scoundrels, but what he did to them is just plain wrong."

"Although," Pop said, "even if it doesn't make it right, they knew who they were playing with when they signed on."

"Birds of a feather," I mused.

"Now what do we do with the captain here?" I asked as everyone glared at him.

He had that *I'm fucked now* look on his face. Old Gus was looking very scared as well.

"Well," Pop said, "he didn't actually try to kill us. He does owe me big time for the damage he's caused the ol' girl here. Besides, until we take care of Nick, he's got bigger things to worry about than us."

"Oh my God, thanks!" he said, wiping his brow and sinking to his knees in supplication. "I'll take care of the damages, and you guys can dive for free from now on."

"Works for me," I said. "You may rise now, slave, and we all drink for free at your bar, too."

"Sure, sure. Anything you say, I'm just so grateful for your mercy," he said as he rose to his feet. Pop and Uncle Jack agreed, then Pop said, "That includes Joe, too."

"And my brother John," Leo joined in.

"You got it," the captain said. "Anything you want."

"Glad you said that," I said. "We're going to need to borrow the *Flo* again. Joe and I want to go back and take some pictures of the grotto with Pop's underwater camera. I also want to get a picture of the two stiffs; it might come in handy when we talk to Nick."

"Good idea," Pop said. "I'll go get the camera."

"Can I come along this time?" the captain pleaded.

I looked at Joe and he agreed. "Yeah, I guess so. But if you try anything, both you and Gus will be swimming back to the mainland," I said sternly.

"Don't worry, I'm done trying anything, and thank you again," he said.

"*Good,*" I said, trying to look mad. I don't think I succeeded.

Just then Pop came up from the cabin and handed me the underwater camera.

"You do know how to use this, right?" he teased.

"*Yes, Pop!*" I responded with an exasperated *you got me* look on my face.

"Payback's a bitch," he said with a big grin.

"Yep. It sure is," I said, starting to laugh.

This brought a round of well-deserved, derisive laughter from everyone, including Captain Pete and Gus. I turned to Captain Pete and said sternly, "You aren't allowed to laugh."

He lifted up his hands as though slightly taken aback and said meekly, "Sorry."

I just smiled then and nodded toward the *Flo*. "Let's go," I said.

You could hear everyone else enjoying the joke as we got on board.

After we returned with our pics of the grotto for our scrapbooks, and some forensic-style photographs of the two dead guys that we hoped to use to blackmail Nick into submission, we were ready to head back to port. We used the *Flo* to tow the incapacitated *Widow* back to San Pedro.

Seven hours later, we were back at Fleitz Brothers. The *Widow* was tied up in her slip, she had been hosed down, and everything put away. We were ready to head home.

"Thanks for your help, you guys," Pop said to Joe, Leo, and Marco. "As usual we couldn't have done it without you."

"No problem," Joe said.

"Yeah, no problem, it was fun," Leo said.

"Yeah, it was great," Marco concurred.

After they all shook hands and left, Pop pulled me and Uncle Jack aside.

"We need to meet up in my office," he said, his tone becoming very serious. "Say tomorrow around ten. That okay with you guys?"

"That's okay with me. How about you Uncle Jack?" I said.

"Ten is fine with me, give us a chance to sleep in a little," he said. "I'll see you there."

Then I asked Pop, "Are you going to file any reports on our incident?"

"No," he said. "We've settled up with Captain Pete. So, no reports to file. No harm, no foul."

CHAPTER 24

A t ten on the nose, I pulled into the parking lot. Pop pulled in right after me. Uncle Jack and Max arrived just as we were getting out of our cars. We all went up to the office together. When we arrived, the office was already open. Jacquie, looking lovely as usual, had arrived early to open up. To our surprise, sitting across from Jacquie was Nick Colleti's younger brother Tommy. I had never met him, but Pop, Uncle Jack, and Max all recognized him right away. He was older than he was the last time any of them had seen him. Well, they too were all older of course. But time had aged the younger Colleti more viciously than the others. He was now gray-haired and slightly hunched over, no longer the intimidating guy he was with a submachine gun in his hands. Prison time had not been kind to him. In fact, I wondered if he could even *lift* a tommy gun anymore. He and Uncle Jack just stared at each other for a long moment.

Then Uncle Jack said, "Hello, Tommy. It's been a long time."

"Yeah, a real long time," Tommy responded. "You too, Frenchy," he said to Pop.

"Not long enough," Pop said sarcastically.

Tommy and Max just nodded at each other, then Max took a seat off to the side, where he just kept a watchful eye on Tommy, as if from habit.

After an awkward silence, Pop said, with a frown, "Maybe it's time we introduced our friend to those of us who haven't had the pleasure?"

Clearing his throat, Jack said, "I'd like you to meet Tommy Colleti."

"Let me guess," I said. "You're here for your share of the loot."

"Hmm, no formalities, cut right to the chase. He must be your kid," he said to Pop.

"You bet. I've trained him well," Pop responded.

"Well, it's a good guess," he said, "now fork it over."

"What makes you think we have it?" I asked.

"A reporter named Lester Sloan visited me in prison awhile back, said he was doing a follow up on the *Rex* heist. Said he and his partners had contacted an old pal of ours about diving for it. So when I got out, I visited our old pal Captain Pete and he gave me the whole lowdown. He promised to cut me in for my share when he had it. So, I thought I'd just visit you guys and collect it in person."

"Good old Lester," I said as we all laughed, much to Tommy's consternation.

"What's so funny?" he asked.

We all looked at each other. "Who gets to tell him?" I asked. "Please let me do it."

"Go ahead," Pop said.

"What's goin' on?" Tommy asked again.

"Well," I said, "it would seem that your dear brother Nick has screwed you too."

"Wadaya mean?" Tommy screwed up his face, and it was hard to keep from laughing again.

We then explained the whole deal to poor old Tommy, and how, while he was rotting in prison, his brother was stealing their stash and opening up his own little gambling joint. Tommy was visibly angry. He stood up and paced the room, then sat back down. We all thought he was going to start breaking things. Maybe even shoot someone; after all, he did have a .38 in his belt.

Pop looked him square in the eye and asked, "You want a little revenge?"

"Wadaya have in mind?" Tommy asked.

"Set up a meeting with your brother," Pop said. "He's going to want to see you. Make it somewhere where we can set up first, in case he wants to take care of you like he did the two Navy guys."

"I know just the place," Tommy said. He then picked up the phone and made the call.

Nick picked it up on the first ring.

"Colleti here," the voice on the other end said.

"Hi, Nick, it's me, your brother," Tommy said.

Silence.

"Ah, hi, Tommy," Nick said. "When did you get out?"

"A couple of weeks ago," Tommy replied. "We need to talk."

"Yeah, about what?" Nick asked with trepidation.

"I think you know. Rumor has it that you didn't go to the East Coast boys to finance your casino, after all," Tommy said. "If it's true and you got the money where I think you got it, I want my share."

"Sure, Tommy, I'll take care of you, like I always have. Just like when we were kids."

"That's what I'm afraid of. I want to meet somewhere private, just you and me," Tommy said.

"Well, where?" Nick asked. "Being an ex-con, you can't show up here."

"Remember that old mine you won in that poker game a long time ago?" Tommy said.

"Yeah," Nick said. "Just north of Beatty."

"Right. That one. Meet me there Sunday at noon. Come alone," Tommy said.

"Sunday, noon at my old mine. Alone. Y—you got it. I'll be there," Nick said shakily.

"Good," Tommy said and hung up.

"It's all set," he said, his voice wavering.

Pop got out a map and spread it out on his desk. We all got up and stood over it. "Show me where this mine is," he said.

Pop and Uncle Jack were very familiar with the Beatty area. Grandpa Harry had served separate terms as the Sheriff of both Beatty and Rhyolite, now a ghost town just southwest of Beatty, before moving to La Quinta in the 1920s. They were bustling mining towns after a big gold and silver strike back in the early 1900s.

"Okay, so this meeting is set for Sunday around noon. You should be there by eight, come hell or high water," Pop said to me. "There's a roadside casino called the Oasis just outside Beatty. You can stay there Saturday night and move into position Sunday morning."

"Sounds good to me," I said.

"Who are you going to get for backup?" Pop asked. "You know Nick won't come alone."

"The usual suspects," I said with a smile. "Leo, Marco, and I should be enough to cover Tommy."

"Okay, that's the plan," Pop said. Then he turned to Tommy and said, "By the way, somebody popped old Lester Sloan with a .38 like the one you're carrying. You wouldn't happen to know anything about that, would you?"

"Nope," he said, "can't help you there. It's news to me."

"Sure it is. Just the same, you'd better stay with Jack so he can keep an eye on you until the meet with your brother," Pop said.

"Okay by me," Tommy said.

"Okay with you, Jack?" Pop asked.

"Do I have a choice?"

"Not really," Pop said.

"Then I guess it's all right with me," Jack said reluctantly.

"Good," Pop said with a smile. "Kit, you line up your crew and pick Tommy up at Jack's on Friday. 'Break a leg' as they like to say in showbiz."

"Copy that," I said.

CHAPTER 25

W e had four days to kill, so I went back to work. Jacquie and I had dinner Wednesday night. As she was grilling the steaks at my place, I asked her if she had decided to tell her mom about Suzy.

"No," she said emphatically. "That's my dad's problem. He and my mom hate each other. They fight every time they get within twenty feet of each other. I'm not going to get in the middle of that. They may not have been dating, much less married, when he had his affair, but it won't matter to my mom. If and when she ever finds out, she's going to want to kill him."

"I guess we'll stay out of it since you put it that way," I said. "But I still don't quite get it. They didn't even know each other when the affair happened."

"You're right, you don't get it," she said. "They really do *hate* each other. Before they were formally separated, they drew a chalk line down the center of the house, dividing their space in two."

"You can't be serious," I said as I started to laugh. "A chalk line, really?"

"I kid you not. It was a literal chalk line. I was so embarrassed. Why do you think I ran off and got married so young? I had to get out of there."

"Wow," I said. "*Now* I get the picture. There is absolutely nothing your father can do that won't bring down the wrath of God from your mom. I think I understand your father a little more. Poor bastard."

"Although it probably wouldn't have made a difference, I think the fact that he just didn't tell her about his past will probably piss her off even more," Jacquie said.

"I hope that never happens to us," I said. "I know you were married before, and I'm sure you've dated other guys before we got together. I want you to know, that doesn't bother me."

"Yes, and I know I'm not the first girlfriend you ever had. It's just . . . Oh, I don't know," she said in a frustrated tone.

"I think I understand," I said. "You want to think that you are special to me, and that I trust you enough to talk about my past. Right?"

"Yeah, I think that's it," she said.

"Look," I said. "Now I know your parents' history, and I get it. But if you're worried that the same thing will happen to us, you can stop worrying right now. You are special and where you're concerned, I'm an open book. Anything you want to know, just ask."

She contemplated that for a second but stayed quiet as she turned the steaks over on the grill.

Then I said, "And as I told you, I'm in for the long haul. I can't think of anyone I'd rather be with than you. I hope you know that."

"I do," she said. "I feel the same way." Then she said, "Your family is so different than mine. I think your mom and dad really love each other."

"They have their fights like any normal couple," I said. "But they always seem to kiss and make up, and I think they always try to not let it drag out. And they do love each other."

"How did they meet?" she asked.

"Well, you know Pop was a patrol cop down in San Diego, before he moved up to LA and became a detective?" I asked.

"Uh huh," she responded.

"Well, just after Kay was born, Mom and her first husband Willie got a divorce. It was the height of the Depression, and she couldn't stay in Florida, so her Aunt Sadie, who ran a laundry in San Diego, brought her out and gave her a job. Since she was just getting on her feet, she couldn't work and take care of a three-year-old too, so she enrolled Kay in the school at the San Diego Mission," I said.

"Boy, that sounds familiar," Jacquie interjected.

"I guess it does at that," I said smiling as I continued, "So anyway, she was visiting Kay one Sunday and it got dark before she could head back to town. In those days, there was nothing but a dark, deserted road between the Mission and the main highway that led back into town. Anyway, she was walking back to the main highway when a police car that was patrolling the area stopped to see if everything was okay—seeing a woman walking in the middle of nowhere—and to see if she needed a ride back to town."

"Let me guess," Jacquie said. "One of the cops in the car was your dad."

"You got it. According to Mom, it was love at first sight on her part. She had just seen a new movie called *Footlight Parade* that had a newcomer named John Garfield in a bit part. Apparently, he made quite an impression on Mom, so when she got in the car and saw my dad, who as Mom tells it reminded her of Garfield, she kinda transferred her 'crush' to Pop."

"Wow," Jacquie said. "Go on."

"Well, as it turned out, Pop was smitten by her as well, and a few days after he and his partner dropped her off at her apartment, he asked her out on a date. And the rest, as they say, is history. When Pop transferred to Los Angeles, they got married and she and Kay came with him. Since Kay never really knew her biological father, Pop has been it, and he embraced her as if she was his own."

"Your dad is quite a guy, taking on a responsibility like that."

"Yeah, he is," I concurred.

"And you take after him," she said. "I think that's why I'm falling for you."

"That's good because I've already fallen for you. Give me a kiss," I said as I grabbed her and pulled her in close.

The steaks were ready, and as we sat down to dinner, Jacquie asked, "So, what's your plan for this weekend's meet?"

I gave her the short version.

"Count me in," she said. "I don't want to miss this."

"Uh, I don't think that's a good idea. Considering how the Colleti brothers feel about each other, it might get dangerous. The last thing I want is to put you in harm's way," I said.

"Well," she said coyly. "You might not have a choice."

"Huh?" I asked. I was guessing there was a surprised look on my face—I wasn't used to having gals tell me up from down. "What do you mean, I don't have a choice?"

"I kinda lied," she said. "Your dad already filled me in on what is going to go down Sunday, and when I told him I wanted to come along, he said it was okay with him. And he's the boss."

"Did he really?" I asked. "You're telling me Pop okayed it?"

This was nuts, and I didn't like it one bit.

"Yes, *really*," she said.

"We'll see about that. Pop and I need to have a little chat about this," I said, still smiling through gritted teeth.

"Won't do any good," she said. "I've already told him I want to become an operative, and I've been practicing on the range, so I can handle a firearm, if that's what's worrying you. He thinks that working with you would be a good way to start my apprenticeship."

"Does he now?"

"Yes, he does, my dear," she responded, reaching out and sliding a finger across my cheek, obviously enjoying my frustration. "Call him up right now and ask him if you don't believe me."

"That won't be necessary," I replied. "I know Pop all too well. This is just the sort of thing he would come up with. I just wish he would've told me what his plans were."

"Don't blame him for that," she said. "I asked him if I could tell you myself. He said 'of course!'"

"Figures," I said, as I started to laugh. "The coward knew how I would react and didn't want to tell me himself." Then I said, "Okay, you're in, but girlfriend or no girlfriend, you'll do exactly as you're told, or you'll sit it out at the motel. You copy?"

"I copy," she said and gave me a peck on the lips.

"As for your marksmanship, I have to confess that Pop showed me your targets. Not bad for a beginner, almost as good as me." I said this, honestly, with an air of pride in my voice. She smiled; I suspect because she already knew it. Actually, she was better than me, but I'd never admit to that, and I'm pretty sure she already knew that, too.

The rest of the week went pretty smoothly. On Friday morning I was at my desk, getting ready for the day's business, when Kathy yelled over to me.

"Hey Kit, there's a guy named Paul on 5. He wants to talk to you."

Paul McPherson was D'Artagnan to Leo's Athos, Marco's Porthos, and my Aramis. The fourth Musketeer. We were "one for all and all for one." As a long-haul trucker, he wasn't around as much as Leo and Marco, so I seldom engaged him to back me up when I was working for Pop. We did try to go camping and sailing as a group at least twice a year, and it was rolling up on the time of year we usually went. That's probably why he was calling, to check in and see if we had plans for this weekend.

"Tall Paul! How the hell are you?" I said. We called him "Tall Paul" because he was six foot four and skinny as a rail.

"Doin' great," he said. "I was just checkin' to see if you and the guys wanted to go camping this weekend; it's that time of year."

"I figured that's what you'd be calling about," I said. "Coincidentally, that's exactly what we are going to do, sort of," I said. "We got a little caper going for my dad, do you want in?"

"Hell, yes!" he roared. "That should be wild!"

I gave him the lowdown on the plan, and what he was in for.

"So, that's the skinny. You still want in?"

"Damn straight!" he replied. "More the ever. This is going to be cool."

"Okay, we'll meet you at the Oasis Motel and Casino around six tomorrow evening."

"I'll be there. You can count on me. I can't wait to see Leo and Marco again." Then Paul quizzed, "So, tell me about your new girlfriend."

"Well, she's twenty-three years old, blonde hair, blue eyes. She's about five foot four, 120 pounds. She kinda looks like Stevie Nicks," I said. "Best part," I added, "is she loves to sail and she's easy to get along with—though she does have a bit of a temper, as I found out the hard way," I said laughing.

"Wow, you lucky bastard. She sounds gorgeous. I can hardly wait to meet her," he said.

"She is definitely gorgeous," I said, "and she's all mine. So don't get any ideas."

"I would *never*," he protested. "You know me."

"Yeah, I do," I said with a chuckle. "That's why I'm warning you in advance."

"Okay, you got me," he said, and with that we both started to laugh.

"I got to go to work—I'm getting dirty looks. I'll see you tomorrow," I said.

"You got it. Tomorrow."

I was just getting ready to take a business call when Kathy yelled at me again. "Leo on 4."

I picked it up and said, "I'm not going to get any work done today if people don't stop calling me. What's up? Oh, and by the way, I just got off the phone with Paul. He'll be joining us tomorrow."

"Crap," Leo said. He sounded disappointed at the news.

"What's wrong?"

"It'd be great to see him again—unfortunately I'm not going to be able to make it this weekend."

"What, why?" I asked, surprised.

"Well . . ." He started to hesitate. "You see it's like this: Suzy and I sort of want to go away for the weekend. You know, just the two of us."

I just laughed. "I get it, you're abandoning your friends in their hour of need for a skirt."

"Aw, come on, you know it's not like that," he protested.

"Just yanking your chain," I said, still laughing. "If things weren't coming down to the wire on this thing, I would probably be doing the same with Jacquie. Oh well, *c'est la vie*. You guys have a good time. I'll be thinking of you when the bullets are flying."

"I'm really sorry. I don't mean to hang you up," he said apologetically.

"No problem. Believe me, I'd rather be off at a beach some-where romantic with Jacquie than doing what we're going to be doing," I said. "I understand and I'm cool with it. Besides, now I've got Paul to fill in for you. Everything works out for a reason."

"Thanks man, I owe you," he said.

"Oh yes, you absolutely do!" I said, starting to laugh again. "And you know I will collect, believe me."

"I know," he said with a chuckle. "I can hardly wait. Stay safe."

"Copy that," I said as I hung up.

Well, it was all set. One way or another, everything was going to be resolved. And it was going to be resolved soon, although what the final outcome would be was not entirely clear at that particular moment.

CHAPTER 26

After work, I picked Jacquie up at her place and she, Marco, and I rendezvoused at Uncle Jack's. I think Jack was more anxious than anybody else to get this show on the road. He'd been sitting on Tommy Colleti for the past four days, and he desperately needed relief from playing nursemaid to the crotchety old gangster and the bad habits he had developed in prison. We got the Bronco loaded and were ready to go.

Uncle Jack said, "You've got two more passengers."

"Who?" I asked, as if I didn't know. Unfortunately, I had a good sense of what was about to come out of his mouth.

"Ray and Debbie are going with you."

"*No. No. A thousand times, hell no.* They'll just be in the way, and I have too much to worry about to have to babysit them too," I said.

"They won't be a bother," he said. "I'm sending Max along to keep an eye on them and remember, these two are still on the hook to Mo Weinstein, so when you work out a deal with Nick, I want their debt to be part of it."

"Uncle Jack, my God, we're not playing *Let's Make a Deal* here. We want Nick to confess to murdering those two sailors on San Nicholas. They don't need to be there."

"They're going," he said, "and that's final. I've already cleared it with your dad. If they give you any trouble, you can shoot them yourself," he snickered.

Nobody laughed.

I groaned.

"Pop is going to get an earful when I get back, if his ears aren't burning already," I said. "First he lets Jacquie talk him into letting her go along, and then he saddles me with these two."

"Cut your old man some slack," Jack said. "He's been doing this a lot longer than you have."

"And?"

"And he knows what he's doing. If he didn't think you could handle it, he wouldn't be letting you ramrod the operation. As for Jacquie, he told me he was going to let her go along to learn the business. He thinks she's a sharp cookie and will make a great detective with the proper training. And he knows she'll be safe with you as her mentor."

"Don't get me wrong, Jack. I appreciate his confidence in me, and you can tell him so when you relay my protest," I said. "It's just that those two have been nothing but a *royal pain in the ass* since I met 'em, and they're just going to be in the way."

"That's why I'm sending Max along. You can let Jacquie help him nursemaid them. That'll be a good way to get her feet wet without being exposed to too much danger on her first time out," Jack explained.

"Hmm, you may have an idea there. She and Max can keep an eye on them while the rest of us deal with Nick at the mine," I said. "But I still don't like it."

Since I had been overruled and I couldn't do anything about it, there was nothing left to do but get underway.

We loaded their gear in with ours. Tommy and Marco rode with Jacquie and me. We headed east toward Vegas. Ray and Debbie followed us in Ray's VW and Max followed in his own car, a beat-up late-model Pontiac GTO that had seen better days. Looking in the rearview, I couldn't rid myself of the thought that it was the sorriest caravan I'd ever seen. Oh well, we certainly looked inconspicuous.

About six hours later, we hit the outskirts of Sin City. Lucky for us, traffic had been light. Normally, on a Friday night, the trip would have taken a lot longer. We stopped at a little diner at the edge of the Strip. After dinner, we decided to find a motel for the night and make the final two hour run to Beatty in the morning.

After breakfast and a refreshing dip in the motel pool, we hit U.S. 95 and headed north. About four in the afternoon, just outside of Beatty, we found the Oasis Casino. It wasn't much more than a wide spot on the right side of the road, fronted by an enormous asphalt parking lot that shimmered in the desert heat, but it had everything. To the left was the bar that doubled as a casino. Next to that was a little Mexican restaurant. There was a driveway that led to the motel in back with a pool across from the main office. On the other side of the driveway was a gas station. Booze, gas, food, lodgings, and gambling. Like I said, everything one needs in life.

Our first stop was the motel office. There were plenty of vacancies; I think most of their business was hourly (okay, so serving the one other thing most folks need in life). Ray and Debbie took one room, Tommy and Max took one—Tommy's absurd demands to have his own room sternly overruled—and Jacquie and I shared another. Marco said he would share his with Paul when he arrived.

We were hungry again, so we tried the Mexican joint. It was a nice little place. A few booths lined the rear and right walls. They had the usual hackneyed Mexican décor, along with pictures of Pancho Villa and other heroes of the *Revolución*. They also had an assortment of serapes festooning the walls and ceilings. The center of the room had tables. The left side of the room had the bar and a door back to the kitchen.

Since there were seven of us, the hostess took us to a large booth in the right corner of the room. When we were all seated, she gave us our menus, left some salsa and chips, and took our drink order. Margaritas were the drink *du jour* for everyone but Tommy; he just ordered whiskey with a beer chaser. While we were perusing the menu, I tried the salsa. In Mexican places, the best indication of how good—or bad—the food is going to be is the salsa. If it's good, then the food probably will be, too. At least that's been my experience.

"This stuff is pretty good. Try it," I said, passing it over to Jacquie for a taste test.

"I'll be the judge of that," she said, stuffing her chip into the tasty red concoction. "Ummm, you're right—this is delicious," she said, going for another taste.

The hostess, who it appeared doubled as our server, was just delivering our drinks. "Is everything satisfactory?" she asked.

"Everything is great," I said with a mouth full of salsa. I took a hit off of my margarita, which was also outstanding, "This stuff is delicious," I said, pointing at the salsa. "We're going to need more of this. And this margarita is fantastic. My compliments to the bartender."

She smiled and said, "Well, since I'm the bartender too, *muchas gracias*."

"*Por nada*," I replied.

"I'll be right back with more salsa and chips," she said cheerfully.

"*Gracias*," I said, wolfing down another salsa-laden chip.

"*Por nada*," she replied as she left.

"If this stuff and the margaritas are any indication of what the food is like, I think we're in for a treat," I said to the others.

"You might be right," Marco said. "This stuff is fantastic."

Tommy looked at us like we were crazy.

"You don't have Mexican food where you come from?" I teased.

He gave me a sour look and said, "I just spent the last twenty years in Folsom, and suffice it to say, we didn't get much variety in our food. And no, back in Detroit where Nick and I came from, they didn't have any Mexicans much less Mexican restaurants."

"They do now," Max chimed in. "We've even got Mexican restaurants in Jersey. Not as good as this, but we've got 'em."

"Then you are in for an experience, Tommy," I said, pushing the chips and salsa over to him. "Try it, you'll love it. And you got to have one of these," I added, pointing to my margarita. "You don't know what you're missing."

"Yeah, try it, you'll love it," Ray echoed.

"He sure will," Debbie said, downing hers in practically one gulp.

"See, someone appreciates it," I said with a smirk.

Another dirty look from Debbie.

Just then our hostess arrived with more salsa and another round of drinks. "Are you ready to order?" she asked.

"Not quite yet," I said. "I think we need a little more time to look at our menus." Everybody nodded in agreement.

"No problem," she said. "Take all the time you want."

With that we all started to peruse the menu. Being a traditional Sonoran-style restaurant, the fare was fairly standard. Enchiladas, burritos, tacos, and the rest. For everybody but poor Tommy, the choices were easy.

"Don't they have any American food?" he asked.

We all looked at him kind of strangely.

"This is a Mexican restaurant," I said, and then I looked to see if there was anything this social cretin might like. Down at the bottom, where most people wouldn't notice, I found something.

"Here you go Tommy. This is your lucky day," I said with a chuckle. "*Quesoburguesa con Papas Fritas.*"

"What the hell is that?" he grumbled derisively.

"A cheeseburger and fries," I said, starting to laugh.

"Ohh," he murmured, starting to catch on. "Okay. That'll do."

"And have a Corona with that," I said.

"What's a Corona?" he asked.

"Boy, you have been away a long time. That's a very tasty *cerveza*," I said.

"Quit screwing with me," Tommy uttered. "What the hell is a *cerveza*?" He looked at me like I'd just stepped off a flying saucer.

"Beer," I said.

"Ohh," he said, as everybody was laughing now. "Fuck you and the horse you rode in on," he said but joined in the laughter.

"Back at you," I toasted, lifting my margarita for a swig.

He just lifted his whiskey glass, nodded smugly, and met the laughter with his own tortured smile.

Just then our hostess arrived. She smiled and said, "I'm glad you're having a good time. Would you care to order now?"

"I believe so," I said as the laughter subsided. We all gave our orders, and when Tommy placed his, he said, "I'll have the cheese *burguesa*? And one of them Coronas."

She looked at him a little quizzically and smiled.

I couldn't help it but I started to laugh again and said, "You'll have to excuse him, he's a gringo."

Tommy just said, "Heh, heh. Very funny." With that everybody burst out laughing again, including the hostess.

She gave me a thumbs up and left to place our orders.

"Sorry man," I said to Tommy trying to control my laughter. "I couldn't help myself."

"It's okay," he said and smiled. I have to admit; his good-naturedness through all of the abuse came as a pleasant surprise to me.

We finally got our dinner—no fault to the hostess, just on account of our jabbering away and skewering Tommy. The food was even better than the margaritas and salsa. I always like it when the food is better than you expect, and when it's this good, you really feel satisfied.

Paul showed up while we were eating dinner. I motioned for him to come over and join us. As he pulled up a chair, I introduced him around. Then I said, "We're just starting dinner. You want to join us? It's on Pop."

"Nah, I'm good. I ate about an hour ago," he said. "But those margaritas look good."

"Cool," I said, and I held up my margarita glass and two fingers for the hostess to see.

She nodded in acknowledgment.

"So how was your trip up?" Marco asked.

"Yeah," I joined in. "Did you have any trouble finding the place?"

"No trouble at all. I took the back roads from Santa Ana, so I avoided a lot of the traffic, and it was no trouble finding this place; it's right where you said it was."

Our margaritas arrived. The hostess—who was proving to be very perceptive—simply brought another round for everyone, even another Corona for Tommy.

"These are pretty damn good," Tommy remarked, holding up his beer. "And this cheeseburger's pretty good, too," he added. Funny, but he seemed to be warming up to the group.

I just smiled and lifted my glass in another toast. He responded with his Corona.

I couldn't help but notice how Debbie's attitude seemed to brighten up when Paul arrived. This girl was something else; just incorrigible. I thought to myself, if Paul played his cards right, he might get lucky this weekend, and I didn't envy old Ray. I could see he was already getting uncomfortable. Paul had evidently noticed that she was staring at him, and the old fox was smiling too, the same way that Sylvester smiles when he sees Tweety Bird. He gave me a quizzical look, nodding his head almost imperceptibly from Debbie to Ray. I just widened my eyes and shrugged my shoulders, as if to telegraph that all was fair game. Maybe I shouldn't have done that, but what the hell. It was going to be a long night.

"Do you want me to get you a room?" I asked. "If you want you can bunk with Marco, he's already offered."

"Yeah," Marco said, "there's plenty of room."

"Nah, but thanks anyway, I got everything I need in my truck," he said, as he wickedly returned Debbie's smile, whom I imagined had seen the inside of a long-haul sleeper cab before. Her grin got even wider and Ray's frown got even worse. It was going to be a long night indeed.

As we wrapped up dinner, Max said he was tired and excused himself. The rest of us went next door to the casino for a drink and a strategy session. Nothing makes for clear thinking better than beer.

The layout was disturbingly similar to a dozen other cheesy casinos that line the Nevada–California border in one-horse towns from one end to the other; places where the out-of-staters could jump across the border, feed their gambling Joneses (and perhaps some other vices) for a few hours, or a debauched weekend, then jump back across, home to their wives and respectable jobs. The huge, well-stocked bar was centered along the back wall. There was the usual row upon row of slots running along the walls, with the center of the floor crowded with a couple of blackjack tables, a craps table, and a roulette wheel, for those who fancied themselves to be serious gamblers. There were also two tables for poker, which I confess mildly interested me, if it weren't for the fact that we were here on business.

Perhaps the most singularly spectacular item in the room—if not the most decadent—was the oversized mural behind one of the poker tables that looked like it came right out of a saloon in the Old West. It was a painting of a voluptuously Rubenesque, scantily clad woman. The general theme of the décor was what you might call "Old West," although with a decidedly Mexicali flavor. Lastly, the Oasis also featured a regulation pool table complete with the classic brass and conical green lamp hanging over it.

These convenient gambling dens, of course, have nothing to compare to Vegas entertainment. However, the Oasis had a section just off the casino filled with tables and booths along the walls for patrons to relax with their drinks and bar food, all arrayed around a decent-sized dance floor, which itself was adjacent to a prominent little bandstand graced by an upright piano.

Ray asked the bartender if he could play the piano; I guess he couldn't help himself, or perhaps he needed a diversion after watching Debbie and Paul ogling each other.

"Knock yourself out," the bartender burbled, a cigarette pressed between his lips. "Our entertainment for tonight got canceled for some ridiculous reason, so the floor is all yours." The cigarette bounced as he spoke.

Ray sat down and started to play. He played the intro to "One More for the Road." If I closed my eyes, I could swear it was Bill Miller playing the intro for Frank.

I turned to Jacquie and said, "Would you like to dance?"

"I thought you'd never ask," she said with a smile. "That song is one of my favorites, and he's actually pretty good."

Pretty good was putting it mildly. Ray was fantastic, and with Debbie obviously on the prowl again, he was really putting his heart into this one. Then he started to sing. He was no Frank, but he gave a very soulful rendition. He'd been down this road before. When he was done, he got a big round of applause from the crowd that was starting to grow. He then started into "Drinking Again," another Sinatra oldie. This time Debbie took the mic. She had a sultry, Dinah Washington sound to her voice. The first time I'd heard Debbie sing was back at Leo's place where I first encountered her and Ricco. That, of course, was amid copious amounts of beer and wine and brandy. Anyway, either I wasn't paying too much attention, or she and Ricco were just fooling around with the music back then, but this time I guess I paid more attention, and, I must say, I was pleasantly surprised. She, too, got a good round of applause.

Jacquie and I were among those applauding, probably a little louder than the rest. She had talent. She and Ray were a pretty good act. I couldn't help but think what a shame it was that they got themselves mired in this difficulty with Mo Weinstein and all the rest of it. We wandered over to the bandstand.

"You were great," Jacquie said.

"Yeah, you were fantastic," I added.

"Thank you. It's nice to know you're appreciated by your audience," Debbie said, glancing over at Paul, who, to the surprise of everyone but me, had apparently circled back to the casino. You could tell he liked what he saw and heard. He was giving Debbie a big grin.

After a few more numbers, a cowboy type dropped a quarter in the juke, and suddenly we were listening to the dulcet sounds of Merle Haggard's "Okie from Muskogee." I was in no mood to start a fight, so I spirited Ray and Debbie off the stage and joined Paul, Tommy, and Marco in a booth. The pool table was free, so Ray, Tommy, Marco, and I split into teams—Marco and me against Tommy and Ray. Jacquie sat on one of the bar-height chairs next to the pool table.

"Ah, the cheerleading squad is here," I said as I gave her a peck on the lips. "Wish us luck."

"Always. But I don't think you need it. Marco already told me how good you are."

He just nodded and gave me a thumbs up.

"Besides, I think there's something going on over there," she said, nodding her head toward Paul and Debbie in the booth.

"You think?" I said with a knowing grin.

"Most definitely." She smiled back with a wink.

Ray was taking notice, too. I wondered if this was going to be a repeat of the incident down at the beach, after that same gathering at Leo's place. I certainly hoped it wouldn't. Although if he knocked himself out again, it might be a good thing. It might make him less of a bother tomorrow.

We lagged to see who would break. I won. Jacquie ordered, "Play ball."

I just smiled and said, "That's baseball, Babe."

She just gave me the finger and smiled.

"Nine ball is the game, rack 'em up," I said to Tommy, who was first for their team.

Marco and I were doing well; we beat Ray and Tommy twice in a row. Although in their defense, I don't think Ray's mind was on the game. I glanced over at our booth. Paul and Debbie were in an embrace in the corner. I don't know who had who in a lip-lock, but it looked really heavy. Of course, Ray was watching all of this, too. He was getting angrier by the minute but not angry enough to start anything. That was a good thing, I knew, because Paul could lay him out flat with one punch.

I could only guess that he'd been through this enough times that he just accepted it now. It was just "Debbie being Debbie." After our game, however, when we rejoined them in the booth, Paul and Debbie were now all over each other.

As they both got up to leave, Paul gave the rest of us a shrug of his shoulders and that plaintive look like, "What can I do?" Ray just looked at them and said to Paul, "Good luck. You'll need it."

That raised everyone's eyebrows, and if looks could kill, Ray would have a knife in his chest and Debbie's prints would be all over it. Then she and Paul disappeared, just like that, without a word from anyone at the table. The rest of us spread out in the booth and ordered some more beer.

"Well. How about them Dodgers?" I said, trying to avoid the elephant in the room.

"Yeah, how about them?" Jacquie replied.

"Do you think they'll get to the series?" Marco said, trying to do his part in trying to lighten things up.

Tommy just looked at us like we were all nuts, and shook his head.

"I know what you're trying to do, and I appreciate it," Ray said somberly.

"It's none of my business," Jacquie said, "but doesn't it bother you what that tramp is doing?"

"Tramp's a little harsh," I cautioned. After all, there was no reason to make Ray feel any worse than he probably did at that moment.

"It's okay, Kit," Ray lamented. "You see, I can't really blame her. She's never said she loves me or anything. She's made it quite clear that we're just friends with benefits and I have no right to be jealous."

"Yet, you are," Jacquie pointed out.

"Yeah, go figure. Am I a dummy or what?"

"Not a dummy," she said. "Just in love."

"We've all been there, man," Marco said.

"Even me," Tommy said, throwing in his two cents.

I couldn't help myself. "Even you? You've been in prison for twenty years," I asked.

"Jesus Christ, I had a life before prison you know! I was married when I got sent up. Little did I know my dime piece was carrying on with someone else. She dumped me the instant I was behind bars," he said, hanging his head.

"Wow, I'm sorry," I said, and, somewhat to my own surprise, I really meant it.

"And I thought my life sucked," Ray said.

We all just looked at him sympathetically.

"I think both of you could use a drink," I said, motioning for the waitress to bring another round.

"Thanks," Tommy said.

"That goes double for me," Ray said.

It was getting late by the time we finished our drinks, and we had to get an early start in the morning, so we called it a night and headed to our rooms. When we passed Paul's truck, it was a rockin' and a rollin'. I didn't need to be a brilliant detective to figure out what was going on inside. We all just shook our heads and dragged ol' Ray back to his room.

CHAPTER 27

I had the office give us a wake-up call for 7:30 a.m. I gave the truck window a good pounding as we passed on our way to breakfast.

As guys will do, I asked, "How was it?"

He just grinned, and I just shook my head.

At breakfast, we finally got around to formulating a plan. The meet with Nick was scheduled for noon and we thought we should get there first and set up. The earlier the better because Nick probably had the same idea. The mine was less than an hour into the foothills. Jacquie and Max were to stay at the motel and keep Ray and Debbie out of the way—and out of trouble, if that was at all possible. Jacquie wasn't too thrilled with that, but when Max explained that this came straight from the top, she reluctantly agreed.

When we arrived, there was no sign of Nick, but that didn't mean he wasn't there already. Fortunately, a little scouting around proved that he wasn't. The plan was for Tommy to wait out in front of the mine entrance for Nick. Since Marco was a big guy at six foot two and about 350 pounds, heavy but agile, we decided he would take a position in the rocks above the entrance. Paul and I would take a position inside the yawning chasm. Tommy was supposed to lure Nick into the mine for privacy, and hopefully get him to spill the beans. Then all of us would close in, in effect, take Nick into custody and deliver him signed and sealed to the authorities. But the plan got shot to hell almost immediately when, no less than ten minutes after we arrived, Ray and Debbie came pulling up the dusty dirt road in Ray's VW followed by Jacquie and Max in Max's car, in a sorry-assed excuse for "hot pursuit." Now these two "entertainers" were really starting to piss me off.

Jacquie quickly exited Max's car, ran over to me, and stammered excitedly, "They slipped away while Max was making a call to your Uncle Jack. I tried to stop them, but they took off before I could draw my gun."

"Shooting them would have been nice, but they're not worth the bullets," I said.

"I'm sorry, man," Max said, as he got out of the car. "I want to wring both of their necks."

"Get in line," I said. "Just keep them as far away from the action as possible and stay out of sight."

"You got it, and again, I'm sorry," he said.

"Forget it," I said. "I probably should have expected this in the first place."

There was no point in trying to get them to go back to the motel and wait, so I didn't even try.

Paul and I started searching around the mine shaft to see if there were any other entrances. We could go in through the main entrance, but we didn't want anyone sneaking in from another way and catching us by surprise. While we were looking, I noticed a local desert rat coming down a trail from a nearby hill. He noticed us too and waved. I waved back and motioned for him to come over; I was hoping he could give us the lay of the land.

"Hi," I said as he approached, "my name is Kit O'Banion and this is my friend Paul McPherson. Do you live around here?"

"Folks call me Cooper," he said as he extended his hand to shake. "Been livin' in these parts for years. Know 'em like the back of my hand."

"Great," I said as I shook his hand. "Do you know if there's another entrance into this old mine other than the main shaft here?"

"This is your lucky day, as a matter of fact I do," he replied, and pointed up to the rocks above the entrance. "Up there is an air shaft that comes in about fifty feet back from the entrance. It's not really an entrance though, unless you was a midget."

"Hmm," I said, "let's go take a look."

It was a rough, sweaty climb over the rocks, but when we got to the air shaft, we saw that it was indeed too small for a normal-sized person to crawl through. That was a good thing. Nick couldn't send his cronies around to get in behind us in case he was planning a little surprise ambush.

"See I told you it wasn't very big," Cooper said.

Then I heard sounds coming through the shaft from inside the mine. It was Marco and Tommy.

"Hey," I yelled into the shaft, "Can you guys hear me?"

"Yeah," Marco hollered through the shaft. The acoustics were remarkable!

"Cool, I just found your position," I called down. "Come on up here and I'll show you."

Then I said to Paul, "This is perfect for Marco. He can see all around the area, and he can hear everything that goes on in the mine. We'll hide close to the air shaft and cover Tommy while he deals with his brother. Marco will stay topside here and be a look-out; he can warn us if we get any unexpected guests."

"Sounds like a plan," Paul said.

It took Marco a while to make the climb up the craggy hillside to the air shaft, but when he finally arrived, I explained the plan to him.

"Cool," he said, "I can survey the whole area from here. So I got your back."

Cooper was listening intently to all of this and getting more curious all the time. Finally, he couldn't contain his curiosity.

"Can I ask what's going on?"

I really didn't want him to know the particulars because he might decide to stick around and get in the way.

"It's an important business deal, worth millions. We are providing security for the parties involved, and we're going to have to ask you to leave. We really appreciate your help," I said.

I think he bought it. "No problem," he said, "I gotta get on back to my place anyway."

We went back down to the entrance and Paul took off to get something from his truck, while Marco and I started to say good-bye to Cooper. I don't know what it is about me, but this happens to me all the time. Sitting at a lunch counter, at a bar anywhere, people just start telling me their life history. As a detective, it does make it easier to get information out of people, but right now I didn't really need it. Just when I thought we were about to get rid of Cooper, he started to tell me and Marco that he hadn't had sex with his wife in years. I thought, *TMI*, and, judging by the look on Marco's face, he was thinking the same thing.

"Gee," I said with strained look on my face, "that must be a little rough."

"Oh yeah, it is, you don't know the half of it," he said.

"You're right," I countered, "and with all due respect, I don't want to know."

Then I added, "You do live in Nevada and there are places right down there where you can find all the female companionship you want," as I pointed toward Beatty, "although it might cost you some."

"You're right," he said, "I may just have to meander down that way tonight."

Just then Debbie and Ray appeared, breathing so heavily from the arduous climb that I feared the two of them were going to need oxygen and digitalis. When Cooper set his eyes on Debbie, the sweat glistening sexily on her bare arms and legs, his eyes lit up, his posture changed, and he had the balls to say, "Mebbe I won't have to go to Beatty after all! I'll give you fifty dollars if you let me have her for an hour."

I must admit, I actually thought about it for a minute, then said, "Nah."

Ray and Debbie were within earshot so I had to crack wise. I said to the guy, "Besides, it's not really up to us. Maybe you ought to ask her. She might say yes. After all, she has had just about all of us, one time or another."

This time it was my turn to get the death look. I'd have to sleep with one eye open tonight, and Jacquie, who was still in hot, hopeless pursuit of her charges, managed to hear the whole exchange. She just gave me a "You're a jerk" look and shook her head. I was going to have to do some serious apologizing tonight.

Max, who had been observing the whole incident, just shook his head and started to laugh. Then he said, laughing even harder, "Your family never ceases to amaze me."

It was getting close to showtime, and we finally got old Cooper to leave—once he realized he didn't have a shot at Debbie. Right on cue, a dust cloud appeared in the distance. We all rushed to our positions, Paul and me racing down the dusty hillside and into the back of the mine, Tommy waiting outside the entrance, while Marco remained at the top near the airshaft. Max had already moved all the cars out of sight, so he and Jacquie got Ray and Debbie out of sight as well. A couple of minutes later, Nick's Cadillac El Dorado pulled up and stopped in a big cloud of dust. When it cleared, Nick got out of the back seat. I assumed that Vic Steckler and Frank Carpo must have made bail somehow, because they too emerged from the Caddy's front driver and passenger seats. I really was not surprised that Nick had brought his muscle with him, and the three men approached Tommy like they were reenacting the scene at the O.K. Corral.

"Hi, Nick," Tommy said guardedly.

Nick acknowledged Tommy and then said, "I guess we both know why we're here."

"Yeah," Tommy said. "Let's go inside the mine. It's cooler in there and a lot more private."

"Okay," Nick said. "Vic, you and Frank stay out here. This won't take long."

"Okay boss," he said.

Tommy walked him to the back of the shaft using a flashlight. It was the perfect location. From where we were, Paul and I could hear everything. It's a good thing I brought my little mini-cassette recorder. So too, hopefully, could Marco at the top of the airshaft.

Tommy opened the conversation. "I want my share. Captain Pete and Black Jack O'Banion were out at the island and they know there is no treasure. What did you do with it?"

"Don't worry," Nick said. "You'll get your share. Don't I always take care of my little brother?"

"Just like you took care of the two birds on the island?" Tommy said.

"Ah," Nick wrung his hands together. "So, you know about that. Hey Tommy, come on. You know how this business goes; people get greedy, they forget their place. So, yeah, I did what was necessary. So now I guess I'll have to take care of you and then go get Pete and Jack."

Just as he said that, he pulled his .45 out of its holster. Paul and I had heard enough. As we jumped out from behind the rocks in the mine, I yelled, "Thank you for your confession. I've got it all right here on tape."

"I guess I'll have to kill you, too," Nick said as he fired.

Fortunately, he missed. Just then, six shots rang out from Tommy's .38, killing Nick instantly.

I just wish he hadn't fired his gun in the mine, though—my ears would be ringing for hours.

Outside the mine, Marco had astoundingly anticipated the events transpiring inside it, and somehow managed to come screaming down the hill in time to get the drop on Steckler and Carpo. Marco ordered them to drop their weapons and raise their hands, but he needn't have worried. As soon as they heard the gunfire reverberating from inside the mine, they took off like scared rabbits, jumped in the Caddy, and tore out of there, spinning tires spewing gravel. All we saw when we came out into the sunlight was another dust cloud heading back toward Vegas. Jacquie, Max, Ray, and Debbie ran up and Jacquie gave me a big hug. Debbie did the same to Paul. Ray just frowned and Max gave us a big thumbs up.

We had Nick's confession on tape, so now I could tell my Navy buddies in NCIS about the two dead sailors on the island without revealing how I knew. I asked Paul if he had his CB radio with him. He did. I had him get on the horn and call the County Mounties. We told them to bring a bus. Nick wasn't going anywhere but the morgue.

They said it would be an hour or so. They were coming down from Tonopah, the county seat. It was about ninety miles away.

"That's okay. I don't think Nick Colleti will be going anywhere," I said.

"Nick who?" the voice on the other end asked.

"Colleti."

"*Wow*," the voice responded. "The boys in Vegas are going to want to hear about this."

"I imagine they will," I said, and signed off.

"Tommy," I said, "they'll probably take you in. Paul and I will testify that it was self-defense—even though you probably didn't have to empty your gun into him."

"I was pissed," Tommy said.

Nick's demise let Ray and Debbie off the hook, so it was over, or so I thought. We had about an hour to get our stories straight. We decided to leave out any reference to the SS Rex and the heist. The loot was gone, and it all happened so long ago nobody could go down for it anyway. The deaths of the two guys on San Nicholas Island were another matter. It was a federal beef, and there was no statute of limitations on murder. But the locals didn't really need to know about that either. I'd have to deal with that later.

Our story was this: Ray and Debbie were on the hook to Nick Colleti. She had told her dad. Since he had done business with the Colletis before, he enlisted the help of Tommy to work things out. Tommy set the meeting up here. It was the truth, sort of. Tommy and Nick got into an argument and Tommy killed Nick in self-defense. Again, the truth, sort of. That was our story and we were going to stick to it. We had no other choice—we would either hang together or hang separately, as the old expression goes.

The sheriffs finally arrived. While they were loading Nick into the coroner's wagon, they searched the crime scene. One of the deputies brought out Nick's .45. It had been fired. One more point in our favor. I asked the deputy if I could look at it.

"Sure," he said.

As I took it from him, it accidentally went off.

"Oops, my bad," I said.

"Be careful with that," the deputy said. "You're lucky it was pointed at the ground, and nobody got hurt."

"You're right, Deputy. I'm so sorry," I said.

Paul and Marco gave me that WTF look. I just shrugged. The sheriffs took our statements and hauled Tommy away in cuffs. They seemed satisfied with our story. They had to take Tommy with them. They'd probably hold him overnight while they did some checking up on whatever facts were still available and let him go in the morning. After they left, I went over to where the gun had gone off and started digging around in the sand.

"Are you crazy?" Paul asked.

"Crazy like a fox," I said as I held up what I was looking for. Held gently between my thumb and forefinger was a nice, freshly fired .45 slug. "I didn't want to go rummaging around in the mine to look for the one Nick fired, so I decided on the next best thing. I'll turn this over to the Navy. Maybe they can match it to the ones rolling around in the heads of those two poor bastards on San Nicholas. Let's get the hell out of here. It's a long way back home," I said.

We piled back into our cars and headed back to the Oasis for a few cold ones before heading for LA.

When we arrived at the casino, we crowded into another booth. "To a successful case," I toasted, as we took our first sip of very cold beer, and very well deserved, in my view of things. *God, that was good!* Nothing like a really cold beer when you're hot and thirsty.

Everyone clicked their glasses, except Ray.

"What's wrong with you?" I asked.

"Nick may be dead, but I'm still on the hook for ten grand. I signed an IOU and it's still in Nick's office. Technically I owe the money to Mo Weinstein, and he will still be able to come after me. I'm not safe until I get that note," he said.

"Well, I guess we've got another stop to make on the way home," I said.

"I'll call your uncle," Max said, explaining, "he wanted me to report in as soon as it was over."

"Cool," I said. "He can call Pop. That'll save me a call."

When he finished his phone call, Max rejoined us and said, "Your uncle wants me to tag along to Vegas. Since I know Mo Weinstein, maybe I can intervene on their behalf for your uncle."

"Not a bad idea," I said. "It'll be different when he finds out Nick is dead."

"That's what your uncle figures," Max responded.

"Okay then," I said, "let's get going."

"Copy that," everybody responded in a kind of down tone.

The Colleti brothers settle up.

CHAPTER 28

The seven of us piled into our respective cars ahead of our journey to Vegas and a rendezvous at Nick's casino. You know, I like to think of detective work as cool and daring; as glamorous and sexy, even intoxicating in a gritty, streetwise kind of way. Like 1940s' film noir where the guys are all savvy and uber-confident and tough as nails—and where most of the knockout women (and they're *all* knockouts) are just as savvy and uber-confident and tough as nails as the guys. But as I stood there with the keys to the Bronco dangling in my hand, standing in the sweltering asphalt parking lot of the Oasis Casino in tumbleweeded Beatty, Nevada, and watching this sorry collection of misfits piling into their dust-covered cars, all I could think of was the movie *It's a Mad, Mad, Mad, Mad World*, and wonder which car Ethel Merman would be getting into.

It was about seven that evening when we arrived. The casino on Fremont Street in beautiful downtown Vegas was typical of the downtown joints. Open to the street, with the sound of ringing slots wafting out onto the sidewalk, as if beckoning the pedestrians inside with the lure of the jackpot. We parked our cars and went in. I patted myself down. I still had my .38 under my jacket. I hoped I wouldn't need it, but it was nice to know it was there. I was also hoping we could do this whole thing discreetly and not have to deal directly with Mo Weinstein.

As we approached the bar, we separated. Paul and Marco took the first two open seats they could that gave them a good view of the casino. Jacquie took Ray and Debbie and found a little booth across from the bar. Max and I looked around to get the lay of the land. Then, lo and behold, we saw our old friends Frank and Vic at the other end of the bar.

"I know those two," Max said. "We go way back to the old days."

"Was your experience with them good or bad?" I asked.

"Neither, really. It was your uncle and Nick that didn't get along. Me and those guys got along okay, but we weren't close."

"Just in case, maybe you should hang back a little," I said. "We don't want them to rabbit again."

"Okay," Max said, "you're running this."

"Thanks," I replied.

While Max found a seat somewhere off in the back, I went over to Vic and Frank to say hello. I made the peace sign as I came up to them. You couldn't help notice the discomfort in their faces when I approached.

"Fancy finding you two here," I said. "I thought you'd be halfway back to New York or Chicago or wherever you're from by now."

"We work for Nick," Vic said. "I don't know what happened back there, but he'll be back."

"Sorry to disappoint you, but Nick isn't coming back," I said. "This place is going to be under new management soon. Any idea who that might be?"

"I dunno," Vic said. "I just work here."

"For now, maybe it'll be your old friend Mo," I said, "and you owe me. Your names weren't mentioned to the Nye County boys. They don't know it was you two who were driving Nick's car, but they'll probably be down to ask a few questions."

"Thanks," Vic and Frank said.

"I know how you can pay me back," I said.

Vic gave me a suspicious look. "Uh huh. And how is that?" he asked.

"You remember Ray and Debbie over there," I said as I pointed over at them sitting in their booth.

"Yeah," Vic said.

"I want their IOU. You know where Nick keeps them?" I asked.

"In his office," Vic said as he motioned to the rear of the casino.

"Shall we?" I said as I tilted my head in the same direction.

We got up and went to the office. It was locked, and neither Vic nor Frank had a key.

"Good luck," Vic said.

"No problem," I said as I whipped out my handy lock pick. Always prepared—a few seconds later we were in.

"Where does he keep them?" I asked.

"In those filing cabinets, but they're locked too," Vic said.

"No problem. One lock is as good as another."

After about fifteen minutes of going through the file cabinets, I found the fat accordion file of IOUs. I decided to grab the whole file.

"I'm taking the whole thing," I said. "I'll go through it when I get home. I'm tired and I just want to get outta here."

"What are you going to do with the rest?" Vic asked.

"I guess they're going to get an early Christmas present," I said. "I'm probably going to burn 'em."

"Nick won't like that," Frank said. Vic and I just looked at him.

"Really."

We locked everything back up and went out to the bar.

"No hard feelings about what happened in the Springs?" I asked.

"No, you was just doing your job like we was," Vic said.

"I admire your professionalism," I said. We shook hands. I gave them my card.

"Look me up next time you're in town. You never know when we'll need somebody with your talents," I joked.

"Yeah, right," they responded with a laugh, then they went on their rounds.

I gathered up Marco, Paul, and Max and we joined Jacquie, Ray, and Debbie in their booth. When we were all seated, we ordered another round of drinks for the road.

Then I said, "Well, I think we're finally done." And I held up the file with the IOUs.

"All right. I'll drink to that," Paul cheered.

"Me too," Marco joined in.

Jacquie just gave me a kiss on the cheek and a big thumbs up.

"Are you sure you got my IOU?" Ray asked.

"As sure as can be," I said. "According to Steckler, Nick kept them all in this file, and he was the only one with access."

"Are you sure?" Max asked.

"I grabbed the whole file, 'cause I didn't want to waste time going through it in Nick's office. I'm going to go through it when I get home."

"What will you do when you find it?" he asked.

"Burn it probably," I said. "Then again, I could just burn the whole file and save myself the trouble of going through it."

"You might get away with destroying one, or even a few of them," Max said. "But if you burn them all, you might piss off Mo and we don't want to do that."

"You've got a point," I said. "I'll just remove Ray's and we can use the rest as a bargaining chip when Uncle Jack works things out with Mo."

"Good idea," Max said, and he lifted his glass in a toast.

"Cheers," we all responded.

We decided we had time for one more round before hitting the road, but Max decided he wanted to head out, so he said his goodbyes and left. The rest of us had one more and then we were ready for the trek home. Ray decided to stay in town and try to find another gig. Debbie just wanted to go home to her dad, so she rode back with Jacquie, Marco, and me. Paul had to go all the way down to Santa Ana, so he said goodbye, gave Debbie a hug and a kiss, and said, "I'll see you later." He said it rather confidently, I thought. As if it were a *fait accompli*. She just smiled.

arco, Debbie, Jacquie, and I piled into the Bronco for the ride home. It would take a while. It was Sunday night, and all the gamblers would be heading back to LA. Most of them would be carrying lighter wallets and purses. Marco took the back seat, folded half of it down, stretched out, and fell asleep before we were out of town. Debbie took the seat next to him, and Jacquie sat up front with me. For the first hour, I had only the sound of the radio to keep me company. After all that had gone down in recent days, I was sort of glad of it. Jacquie had fallen asleep too, and Debbie was giving me the silent treatment.

Finally, she said, "I'm still mad at you."

"For what?" I asked.

"Those things you said to the old guy out at the mine."

"I was joking," I said.

"Well, it wasn't funny," she said.

"Well, you could hardly blame me," I said. "It was a reasonable comment. Let's recap. You show up in Manhattan Beach with Ray, who you were sleeping with. You make a pass at me, and when I politely decline your generous offer, you wander off with Dirk. But you weren't done there, because then you ended the evening hooking up with Leo. Now you're doing the deed with Paul. If fact, right now I'm trying to think of a guy you *haven't* hit on through this whole ordeal. So it wasn't much of a stretch to think you might take care of the old guy."

She just sneered.

"Besides," I said, "a lot of people have gone to a lot of trouble to get you and Ray out of a jam. We almost got ourselves killed more than once. We were only doing it because you're family, and you can't even say thank you. I'm the one that should be angry."

She thought about that for a minute, and then said, "Sorry. Pax," as she held out her hand.

"Pax," I said as I shook her hand.

A little more silence.

"Would you have done it if I wasn't family?" she asked.

"Hell, yes," I said, "but it would have cost you big time. We don't work cheap."

"Oh," she said, and we both laughed.

About four hours later we were home. I dropped Debbie off at Uncle Jack's, filling him in on what happened. Told him I would tell Pop tomorrow. After dropping Marco off at his place, I took Jacquie home.

On the way she said, "I forgive you."

I said, "Oh, yeah?"

"Yeah, I wasn't totally asleep on the way to LA. I heard your conversation with Debbie. After hearing all of her escapades since you met her, I understand why you said what you did to that prospector. You are a smart-ass and that is what I'm forgiving you for."

"Thank you. I appreciate it and I apologize to you."

"You're welcome," she said. "By the way, your mom and pop are watching Nick and Fred, so we'll be all alone when we get home. That is if you want to stay."

She didn't have to twist my arm. As we arrived, the Sheriffs' mounted posse was lining up again for their nighttime practice routine. Jacquie changed into something comfortable while I grabbed a Michelob out of the fridge and poured her a Merlot. When Jacquie came back, she was wearing the shirt I gave her and nothing else. That's what I call comfortable.

She put *Bolero* on the stereo and said, "I understand it is one of your favorites."

"It is," I said, as we clinked our glasses and snuggled up on the couch.

The music started building up to its inevitable crescendo. Just as it reached its peak, we heard the mounted posse parading by in front of her open window. I had always thought *Bolero* conjured an image of marching armies approaching from the distance and being right in front of me when it reached the end. The sound of the horses' hooves hitting the pavement completed the image. These days, I think I will forever associate the sound of those horses with that point in the song every time I hear it. We fell asleep on the couch, in each other's arms as usual. This was getting to be a habit, and a good one at that.

CHAPTER 30

L uckily, I woke up just early enough to rush home and get ready to go to work. I had thought about what to do with the file I took from Nick. I left it with Jacquie to take to the office. I asked her to find Ray's IOU and give the rest to Pop, to let him and Uncle Jack decide what to do. On my first break, I made a couple of phone calls. The first was to Pop's office. Jacquie answered. It was so nice to hear her voice. It had only been since I kissed her goodbye that morning, but it seemed like forever. In all the chaos, it was comforting to know she was around and was hopefully going to be a new constant in my life.

I made a date with her for dinner, and then she transferred me over to Pop.

"Thanks for sending the file in with Jacquie," he said. "We found Ray's IOU in there."

"Great," I said. "What are you going to do with the rest?" I asked.

"I'm going to give them to Jack. Since he knows Mo Weinstein, he can use them as a bargaining chip. I think he has plans to make a move on Nick's casino," he conjectured.

"That doesn't surprise me," I said. "Even if Tommy were to inherit it from Nick, he can't operate it because he's a felon. And never mind he's also pretty incompetent to do anything like that. And Uncle Jack has always been able to turn a crappy situation into an opportunity."

"That's my brother," Pop said with a chuckle. "I imagine your version of the weekend's events will match up with Jacquie's, so I'm just going to have her type up a copy for her to sign and one for you. If you want to add anything after you read it, you can."

"Cool," I said. "I'm going to call my old CO at NCIS and tell him about the two dead Navy guys on San Nicholas. I'm sure they'll be very interested to know."

"Don't be too specific on how you know about them," he said, his voice turning a bit more serious.

"Don't worry, I've already figured out how to tell him without giving it away that we were on the island."

"Not just that," Pop said. "You don't want to implicate yourself in any way in that."

"As far as the Navy is concerned, the trip to the island never took place," I said.

"Anyway, come to the office after work. Fat Al has called a meeting to coordinate our stories, and to deal with any loose ends," Pop said.

"Like, Lester Sloan?" I asked.

"Yeah, like Lester Sloan," he responded.

"Okay Pop, I'll be there. I gotta make that other call and go back to my real job."

He just laughed and said, "Copy that."

My next call was to the Federal Building. NCIS has an office there. I was attached to NCIS for my last year of active duty. Because of my detective background, it was a natural assignment. I spent my last year doing background checks on potential officer candidates. Yeah, it was a real thrill—not. My old boss, Commander McConnell, was still in charge.

"Hi, Mac," I said when he picked up the phone. "I've got some brownie points for you."

"That'll be the day," he said. "How's tricks? You keepin' out of trouble?"

"If I were, I wouldn't be calling you," I said.

"I guess not. What d'you got?"

I filled him in on the whole *Rex* deal, and Nick's part in it. Then I said, "You've got a couple of dead sailors in a cave out on San Nicholas. Nick killed them. I've got his confession on tape, and a slug from his gun. It just might match the ones in your dead sailors."

"How did you find out they were on the island?" he asked.

"I'm not really at liberty to discuss that—it sort of came up in the course of an investigation into another matter," I said.

"Yeah, right," he said. "Well, thanks for the tip. Stay out of trouble. If you can. Oh, and drop that slug and confession off at my office. Where can I get you if I've got more questions?"

I gave him my work number.

"Later," he said and hung up.

Well, that took care of that. Break over, back to work. I'd edit the tape later.

CHAPTER 31

The rest of the day was business as usual. At quitting time, I left the office as fast as I could get out of there. All I wanted to do was hold Jacquie in my arms again. But first, there was the meeting at Pop's office.

I arrived at 3:30 p.m. on the nose. Jacquie was at her desk typing up our reports. I got a great big smile from her when she saw me. I returned the smile and walked over to give her a kiss. She gave a slight chuckle and said, "You don't have time for that now." And motioned to the door to Pop's office. "But hold on to that thought."

"Will do," I said. "You can count on it." Then I went into Pop's office.

All the usual suspects were there. Pop was seated behind his desk, Fat Al and Uncle Jack were seated directly across in two of the club chairs, and Max was occupying a third toward the side of the room. The remaining chair had been reserved for me.

"Grab yourself a beer and take a seat, we've been waiting for you," Pop said.

I got my drink, lit one of Pop's Cohibas, and sat down.

Then Pop said, "Okay, let's get down to business. I think we all know why we are here. We've taken care of Jack's little blackmail problem, and we've taken care of Ray Ricco's little debt problem with the late Nick Colleti. We've also resolved the mystery of the robbery on the *Rex* so many years ago. All in all, quite successful. But . . ."

Here it comes, the other shoe was about to drop.

"But," he continued, "there is still this loose end in the matter of Lester Sloan. We still don't know who shot him, and I also find it very strange that the police have not followed up on Kit's appearance at Lester's apartment. After all, it's been over four weeks since it happened."

"I've been wondering about that too," I said. "I was too involved in all the other stuff to really think about it."

Then Fat Al, who had been listening intently to our discussion, spoke up. "Actually, gentlemen, the matter of Lester Sloan's death has, in fact, been resolved. The police have ruled it justifiable homicide and closed the case."

There was such complete silence in the room, you could hear a pin drop. But it seemed that only Pop and I had surprised looks on our faces.

Then Pop took a deep breath and said, "What the hell, Al, would you mind filling us in on the details, since it appears that Kit and I are the only ones who don't know anything about this?"

"I can explain with just two words," Al replied. "Plausible deniability."

"Not enough, Al!" Pop said, nearly shouting and starting to show his anger and frustration.

"I'd like to know more too," I said, mirroring Pop's anger.

"I can explain now that the entire matter is settled," Al said.

"Go on," Pop shot back.

"As your attorney, both on behalf of you personally and for your agency, it is my duty to protect you as much as possible. Therefore, the less you knew about the actual circumstances of Mr. Sloan's death the better. After all, Kit had already informed the police that Sloan had hired your agency to do some background investigation on a story he was writing. I took it upon myself to adjust the call logs to provide backup for Kit's version of what happened and inform the police that any contact with Kit needed to be arranged through me. They were satisfied with the evidence I presented, and he was dismissed as a suspect."

"Okay, that gets me off the hook, but just who the hell killed Lester?" I asked, getting really frustrated now.

"I'm getting to that," Al said. "After you expressed your concerns over how simple the exchange was going to be, Jack and I started thinking about that, and we decided to send Max here to follow you. He arrived at the location on Mt. Washington before you did and was able to keep both himself and his car out of sight.

"When Sloan fired his two shots at you, he apparently thought he was shooting at the same thugs who had roughed him up earlier that same afternoon. We can't know for certain, but Sloan may have feared they were coming back to finish the job, so to speak.

"So, in any case, Max shot Sloan. I was able to devise a plausible story as to why Max was there. I told the police that he was there on a personal matter for my client, your uncle, and was unaware of the identity of Sloan. Since it was in self-defense, his only real crime was leaving the scene of the incident. I was able to have that charge dropped."

"Wow," Pop said.

"I'll second that," I said.

"You are good," Pop said.

Fat Al just smiled, rolled back in his chair, and said, "That's why, as you say, I get the big bucks."

"Well, I'm still a little pissed," I fumed. "We've had at least three meetings where the subject of Lester Sloan came up, and you never said a word. I've accused everybody from Ray and Debbie to Nick's boys Vic and Frank. I've been racking my brain trying to figure a way to nail one of them. What a colossal waste of time that's been! It would have been nice if you'd filled us in."

"Again, plausible deniability. The less you knew, the better."

"Yeah, you're probably right, but I'm still pissed," I said, starting to smile.

"Duly noted," Al replied.

Pop just shook his head and said to Al, "We need to work on our communication." Then he looked at Uncle Jack, who had been uncharacteristically silent through all of this, and said, "You too, Jack!"

Uncle Jack didn't say a word. He just nodded in agreement and sat back in his chair.

"Hey, Uncle Jack, what are you going to do with the rest of the IOUs I swiped from Nick Colleti's files?"

"I'm going to use them to negotiate with Mo Weinstein and clear up a few matters regarding Tommy," he said.

"Anything else?" I asked.

He just smiled a Cheshire cat smile and said, "None that concerns you."

I just said, "Uh huh."

"Well," Pop said, "I guess that wraps it up. Thank you, Kit, you did great work. Tell Leo, Marco, and Paul I appreciate all their help, and that appropriate compensation is on the way."

"I'll relay the message; I'm sure they'll appreciate it," I said. "Catch you later, Pop, but now I have more important things to take care of," motioning toward the outer lobby.

"Call your mother," he ordered, with a smile.

"Will do, Pop. Love you."

"Love you too," he said.

Then I turned to Max. "Thanks. I really owe you one."

"That's okay. You'd do the same for me."

"Copy that," I said.

We shook hands, and I said goodnight to Pop one more time as I left. Fat Al, Uncle Jack, and Max stayed behind, probably to discuss Uncle Jack's plans to deal with Mo Weinstein. I'd be willing to bet that Pop would also be giving Fat Al and Uncle Jack an earful about not telling us what was going on.

Jacquie was still at her desk. She looked at me and asked, "Well, what happened?"

"I'll tell you later; you're not going to believe it, but everything is cool. All I have to do is sign those reports that you've typed up and we're done. "

"We'll talk about it over dinner," she giggled, "I can't wait." She grabbed her purse and jacket and we left.

CHAPTER 32

Dinner was a quiet one at my place. She had made a stop at Ralph's on the way home and had all the fixings with her. She had some more of my Czech beer with her as well, which she had five-fingered out of the fridge in Pop's office.

"Where did you get that?" I asked. "We should have run out of that a long time ago."

"Well," she said, "your dad knows a guy who knows a guy, and well, about four cases showed up in our office this morning. I iced some down for tonight. I put it in my car while you were in the meeting."

Gotta love Pop and his connections. I was going to have to make sure at least one of those cases ended up in my refrigerator. I got into my casual clothes while she prepared dinner. She had the hibachi fired up and was grilling some chicken. I do eat something besides steak, believe it or not.

When I told her what went on in the meeting and that the case was finally over, all she could say was, "No shit, Max shot Lester Sloan?"

"Yep. Fat Al and Uncle Jack sent him along as backup when I complained about how easy they were making it out to be," I said. "I guess they started to get concerned about it themselves. Anyway, looking back, I'm damn glad they did."

"Me too," she said with a smile and hug. "I'm just getting used to having you around."

"Well, I'm getting used to being around too, and liking it," I said responding with a kiss.

"I'm glad things worked out," she said, and changed the subject. "By the way, I talked to my dad. He said he told my mom about Suzy and that he was going to acknowledge her as his daughter."

"I'll bet that went over well," I said, only slightly kidding.

"I can't say with certainty, because he didn't let on as to how it went. But according to her neighbors they could hear her screaming all up and down the block."

"Sounds like she took it better than I expected. At least she didn't hit him with a frying pan or something," I joked.

"Real funny, asshole," she said to me with a smile and a kiss on the cheek. "You didn't have to grow up with those two fighting all the time."

"Well, I kinda got a general idea when you told me about the whole chalk line thing. It must have been hell," I said.

"They're the reason I ran away and married Nick's father, Terry." She said, "I absolutely love Nick so I can't really regret it, but, oh boy, on all other counts, what a mistake that was!"

"I'll bet," I said, and gave her a big hug. "Must be tough being a single mom and all."

"Yeah," she said. "It has its ups and downs." Then she asked, "Does it bother you at all that I have a two-year-old child to raise?"

"Not in the least. When we got back together again back in La

Quinta, I knew you had a kid then. It didn't bother me then and it doesn't bother me now."

"That's reassuring," she said with a smile and kiss on the cheek.

"Also, do you remember that night we had our little talk, the first time we actually spent the night together, and I told you that I didn't know what the future held but that I was in it for the long haul? Well, I meant it then, and now that the future gets clearer every day, I mean it even more. I love you, Jacquie."

"I love you too," she said as she gave me a great big kiss and hug.

We enjoyed our dinner and spent the rest of the evening cuddling and listening to music. As usual, we fell asleep in each other's arms.

CHAPTER 33

The next few weeks flew by, and a lot happened during that time. Fat Al, it seemed, was worth every penny Uncle Jack and Pop paid him. In addition to his handling of the whole Max–Lester Sloan thing, Fat Al also convinced the Nye County DA not to press charges against Tommy Colleti for violating his California parole by having a gun. The shooting of his brother Nick was ruled self-defense and he walked. Fat Al was also able to prove that Tommy was rightful heir to Nick's assets even considering the questionable circumstances of Nick's demise. However, since he was a convicted felon, the Nevada Gaming Commission refused to let him even go near the casino he inherited from his brother.

That's where Uncle Jack found the opening he was looking for. Pop's instincts about his brother were spot on, because Jack convinced Tommy to sell any interest he had in Nick's casino to him. Then he confronted Mo Weinstein, using the fat accordion folder of IOUs as a bargaining chip, no pun intended. Mo figured that half of something was better than all of nothing, so he and Uncle Jack worked out a little profit-sharing plan, to take effect as soon as Uncle Jack had control of the casino. He still held a Nevada Gaming license from the old days, so he had no trouble with the gaming commission.

Sometimes everything just works itself out. Tommy got his share of the spoils in the form of a buyout. Ray was off the hook to Mo Weinstein, and Uncle Jack gave him a gig playing piano in one of the lounges, under the condition that he stayed away from the tables. Max followed Uncle Jack to Vegas and took his girlfriend with him. Uncle Jack put him in charge of security. Vic Steckler and Frank Carpo would now work for Max. I don't know, maybe Uncle Jack and Max thought the two bumbling goons could be rehabilitated, or maybe they just figured that, with proper supervision, Vic and Frank could be managed to "do no harm." In any case, all was well in Sin City.

A couple of weeks after the dust of our latest caper together had settled, I called Paul to say hey, just to check in on him and say thanks again. Debbie answered his phone. It seems that Paul had wasted no time in getting Debbie ensconced in his place. He and Ms. Long, my newfound cousin, had already been to my Uncle Jack's house, picking up her stuff. Jack had given her the large manila envelope that included the articles that "very much exaggerated the reports of her mother's death," as Twain might have put it. Anyway, I wished them both luck and I was sincere. Then I asked her to have Paul call me. I've yet to hear from him, but that is just the way it is. Hopefully he'll come up for air in time for the next caper, should I need him.

———

The day was fast approaching when Suzy would be obliged to return to London. I wanted to do something celebratory to mark the occasion of her cross-training visit with us and all that we learned from that. But a whirlwind of activity at work demanded my attention, at least for the moment.

On Wednesday, I got called into the office of my boss, a tough-minded, yet reasonably amicable, guy by the name of Dick Lane. *What now*, I thought. When I got there, already seated with Dick were Artie Johnson and Mori Ogawa, essentially the triumvirate senior management team for the Foreign Exchange Trading Department of Security Pacific National Bank—all heavy hitters.

Dick said, "We've been doing a little reorganization and we feel that you are just the man to head up a new desk. We've decided to consolidate the middle market development and the regional banks under one desk. We think you are the person to head that up."

"Wow," I said.

"And to make it a little more interesting," he said, "there is a promotion and a nice raise to go with it."

Another "wow" from me.

"Then congratulations. You are now an assistant vice-president," he said and handed me the formal letter. "Your new salary is described in the letter. We are hoping you find it—as well as the accompanying benefits—more than satisfactory."

"Okay," I said, a little speechless as I shook everyone's hand.

"You can go back to work now. We'll discuss the details later. Send Kathy in. She's going to be working with you, so don't say anything."

"Gotcha."

I told Kathy they wanted to see her too.

I just said, "It's all good," when she asked me what was going on.

I sat down at my desk as she headed to Dick's office. I could hardly wait to get the envelope open. When I saw the figure mentioned, all I could say to myself was "*Far out!*" It was good. I was now in the upper five figures. "Wow," I repeated, stunned at my good fortune.

I immediately called Jacquie and she picked up on the first ring.

"Triangle Investigations, Jacquie speaking, how may I help you?" she practically crooned. I loved to hear her talk on the phone. She gave great phone.

"Hi, Babe," I said in a very happy tone. "We're celebrating tonight. I have some great news."

"What?" she asked.

"I can't tell you over the phone, there are too many ears around. You'll have to go with '*It's great!*' for now."

"It must be, I can tell by the sound of your voice."

"It concerns Kathy, too. Do you mind if I invite her and Ron along, if they're available, I mean?"

"No, not at all. I can hardly wait," she said. "I got to run—your dad's calling me into his office."

"Okay, Kathy is coming out of Dick's office right now and she has a big smile on her face too. I'll call you later. Love you."

"Love you too," she said as she hung up.

As Kathy sat down, I could tell by the expression on her face that the letter in her hand was filled with similarly good news.

"Well, what do you think of the new situation?" I asked.

"What do you think?" she said as she waved the letter over her head, her smile getting bigger and bigger. "I have to call Ron and give him the good news. We've got to celebrate tonight."

"I thought you might want to do that. How would you and Ron like to join Jacquie and me at Damon's tonight, say around seven o'clock? My treat," I said.

"I'd love to. I'm sure Ron will too."

"Cool, it's a date."

That night, we all met for dinner. We asked Suzy to join us, though I admit that I felt a little guilty at hoping to make the dinner double as a kind of bon voyage for her as well. Not that Suzy would have asked for anything more. Fortunately, she was free and able to come along. Okay, I admit I was also glad that now the dinner would be on the bank; I'm just being pragmatic, that's all. Anyway, we all shared our good news, without discussing salary, of course, although I got the impression that Kathy's raise was excellent as well. She was made international officer and my assistant on the new desk.

After a toast of Dom Perignon, things quieted momentarily, and Suzy seized the opportunity. "I have a little announcement of my own," she teased. "As you may know, with Kathy's promotion, the clerk spot is open, right here in the home office. Dick offered it to me. It seems that was why they brought me here in the first place. To look me over, I guess," she joked, then laughed at her own joke.

"And you're taking it, right?" Jacquie interjected excitedly, unable to keep the eagerness from her voice.

"Of course I am," Suzy said. "I'd be a fool to leave my new family right after having found them."

"That old dog," I said. "Here's to Dick."

Tears welled in Jacquie's and Suzy's eyes.

We all lifted our glasses and said, "To Dick."

Suzy continued, "I still have to go home and get things in order, but I'll be back in a couple of weeks. This is so wonderful. The new job is wonderful enough, but that doesn't hold a candle to the fact that now I have a family. And that also means they don't need to get me a work visa anymore"—Suzy paused as she placed her hand on one of Jacquie's—"I can get a green card since Jack—I mean, our father—has agreed to sponsor me as a family member."

"To Jack!" I said.

"To Jack," was the unanimous response, as we toasted once again.

It seemed as though everything *does* work out perfectly. Maybe not every time, but certainly some of the time. After all the helter-skelter, things were all good. All good indeed.

CHAPTER 34

On Friday, Leo called to inform me that he was throwing another of his signature parties that Saturday, and that Jacquie and I were invited. Yeah, Leo wasn't known for giving a lot of notice.

"I'm bringing some friends," I said. "If that's cool."

"The more the merrier," Leo said.

"Have you talked to Suzy? I know you two have been seeing a lot of each other these last few weeks," I asked.

"Yeah, she gave me the good news about being transferred here," he revealed.

"Great, I'm guessing she will be there as your date, so I won't have to invite her along," I said.

"You got that straight. See you tomorrow," he said as he hung up.

Good. Now we had a nice party to go to for Suzy's last night in town.

Jacquie and I arrived fashionably late, around nine. We brought Ron and Kathy along with us, arriving just as Marco pulled up. I hadn't seen the gang in a while, so it was nice to see them again. After introductions were made all around, we grabbed some drinks and started to mingle. Leo and Suzy came over to join us as soon as they spotted us. After a little small talk, Suzy and Leo decided to dance. That sounded like a good idea, so Jacquie and I decided to join them.

I said, "I think Suzy's going to be living at the beach when she returns. What do you think?"

"You could be right," Jacquie responded with a smile. "They have been seeing a lot of each other, and Suzy confided in me that she really likes him."

"Well, I have it on good authority that he feels the same way about her."

"I'm glad to hear that. They go well together."

"Yes, they do. They are a lot like us," I suggested.

"Oh yeah?" she asked coyly. "In what way?"

"Well, he's obviously in love with her, and she with him. You know I'm in love with you," I said, "and you're in love with me. Of course, I also love Nick, too."

"I know you do, and that's part of why I love you too."

Then she said with a laugh, "I guess we could move in together too, but I don't think three of us could fit in your little, one-bedroom apartment."

"That's an easy fix," I said with a knowing smile. "That two-bedroom unit next door to mine just became available. The landlord said I could have it if I wanted it."

"You asked him about it?" she asked.

"Yeah, of course. At first, I was just curious about it, but you know me, I always like to be prepared."

"Prepared for what?" she asked with an accusative chuckle.

"Oh, I don't know, maybe just in case you asked me to live with you," I said with the old Cheshire cat smile.

"In that case, I'm asking," she said.

"Well, I don't know," I said, rubbing my chin as if pondering, "I'm awfully fond of my apartment."

"*What!?*" she blurted, a little taken aback by my response.

"*Just kidding!*" I said. "Of course I'll move in with you. I can't think of anything I'd like better."

"Good answer," she said, and she too had a Cheshire cat smile.

Just then Suzy and Leo walked up. When she saw the big grins on our faces, Suzy asked, "You two look happy, what's going on?"

"Yeah, something's going on. What's up?" Leo joined in.

"We'll tell you later," I said. "Trust me. It's all good."

———

We all had a wonderful evening, but soon it was time to call it a night. After all, we had to get Suzy to the airport in the morning. Leo had, shall I say, *simplified the logistics* by graciously helping Suzy bring all of her things to his place, most of it already packed in suitcases ready for the airport. Such a devil—he also said that he volunteered to take her to the airport in the morning—such a *gracious* devil.

"Okay with me," I said. "But we'd like to see her off too. Why don't we all go down together?"

"Agreed," Leo confirmed. "Seven o'clock—sharp, okay?"

"Copy that," I said with a wink and a smile. "You two have a pleasant evening."

"You too," he responded with a smile and a thumbs up.

Suzy just smiled, basking in the glow of new family and new friends and new more-than-friends.

Jacquie and I went to my place to have our own good evening.

The next morning, we were up early. We swung by Jacquie's place so that she could change clothes. She threw on a clean pair of jeans and a white tee, and then we were off to Leo's place by the beautiful beach. Suzy was dressed in a smart-looking camel-colored suit, ready for the business-class section of the plane. You gotta hand it to Security Pacific Bank, they do things in style. We got Suzy safely aboard her plane. We said our goodbyes, knowing it would only be a couple of weeks and we'd be back here, happily picking her up for good. She and Jacquie shared hugs and kisses. I gave her a kiss on the cheek, and then she turned to Leo. Their very warm goodbye just confirmed Jacquie's and my suspicions.

She would most definitely be living at the beach when she returned.

It was still very early in the morning when Suzy's plane left the tarmac at LAX, so the three of us decided to grab a light breakfast at the airport before heading home. After that, Jacquie and I just chilled the rest of the day, doing those usual things that couples do, when all they really want to do is just to be together, no plan needed. You know, like shopping at the mall. When we were done whiling away the afternoon, we were perfectly content to go out for a light, quiet, low-key dinner together, just the two of us, and we didn't get to Damon's until nearly 10:00 p.m.

CHAPTER 35

By the time we finally got back to Jacquie's apartment, it was already after midnight. The Sheriff's mounted unit was lining up as usual for their nocturnal maneuvers.

She invited me in. "We can watch them parade from my window," she said.

Even though tomorrow was another workday, I didn't mind. Being tired in the morning would be worth it. She instructed me to grab a beer and pour her a glass of Merlot. I am good at following instructions. Sometimes.

Much to my delight, some of my Czech Michelob had made its way into her refrigerator too. I went into the living room and opened the window to let some cool night air in. I kicked my shoes off and made myself comfortable on her couch. When she came in, she was wearing my shirt and a smile again.

"Get comfortable," she said, as she put a record on the stereo. It was *Bolero*. By the time she was sitting next to me, I had already begun to be mesmerized by the melody. We cuddled up on the couch and listened to the slow crescendo rising to its inevitable climatic flourish. Jacquie just smiled. Then . . . there were the horses.

It felt good, knowing this was just the beginning.

Just the beginning . . .

ABOUT THE AUTHOR

LARRY O'BRIEN was born in Glendale, California, and raised in Eagle Rock, a neighboring suburb of Los Angeles. There he graduated from Eagle Rock High School. After high school, he got a job in the mail room of Security Pacific Bank and worked his way through college while serving in the United States Naval Reserve. He eventually graduated from California State University Long Beach and transferred to the International Banking Department where he rose to the position of assistant vice-president as a foreign exchange trader. When the bank merged with Bank of America in 1991, the author and several of his colleagues were encouraged to seek other employment. Twenty years and several other employment opportunities later, he retired. Through a mutual acquaintance, he met the renowned private investigator and author Nils Grevillius. Nils offered Larry the opportunity to obtain a private investigator's license through his tutelage. Larry did just that and has worked off and on for Nils ever since. It was Nils's writing efforts that inspired Larry to write his first novel, *Cornero's Gold*.

Larry still lives in Glendale, California.

ABOUT THE ILLUSTRATOR

LIAM O'BRIEN was born in Hollywood and raised in Glendale. After graduating from Hoover High School and doing a year of undergrad work at Pasadena City College, Liam transferred to Los Angeles Trade-Technical College where he studied plumbing and received his certificate in the field. After a couple of years digging ditches in the hot sun, Liam decided to return to Glendale Community College where he finished his first two years and then attended California State University Northridge to study art and animation. A sample of his work is represented in *Cornero's Gold*. Liam currently lives in Glendale, California.